Jeopardy

'Silence can be deafening but the truth is even louder'

Acclaim for Jeopardy

"...the narrative voice is strong and convincing with a clearly identifiable viewpoint. If we've all got a book in us, I think this is his"!

"My overall view of the book is that it has a captivating storyline and it kept me interested as I wanted to know what happened".

"I have enjoyed the plot and the writing is better and adds suspense as he gets in the tale".

"So I really enjoyed the book. The last few chapters kept me very captivated - I stayed up late because I wanted to find out what had happened the other night - unheard of for me".

"...believable characters and succeeds in highlighting problems within modern policing, from lack of funding to endemic corruption".

Jeopardy

In an age of austerity cuts to the police are having a profound effect, but the drive for promotion knows no bounds. The use of informants has never been under such scrutiny by a sceptical public.

Can their use be justified, even when it helps combat the abuse of power and corruption?

Nick Inge

This book is dedicated to the downfall of those
who think that they can get away with it

Also by Nick Inge
Exposing the Truth
Whistleblowing Uncovered

Learn the Secrets of Speaking-up

Exposing the Truth – Whistleblowing Uncovered is a comprehensive guide for those thinking of embarking on the whistleblowing journey, for those just starting on it, and for those who have come out the other side.

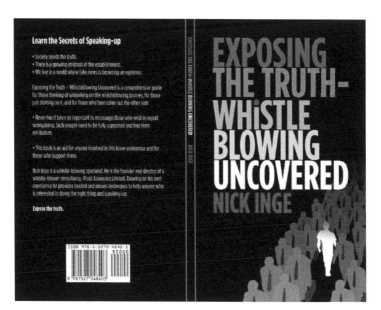

About the author

Nick Inge spent over 25 years in the police, nearly 20 of which were working in covert policing. He has managed people who have provided information about acts of criminality ranging from shoplifting to terrorism. He knows from personal experience what it takes to lift the lid on those committing wrongdoing and the journey that needs to be undertaken.

Using his extensive experience, he founded a whistleblowing consultancy, iTrust Assurance Limited. iTrust Assurance Limited acts as an independent third-party that enables the voices of those with knowledge of wrongdoing to be heard in a safe and non-judgemental environment and aims to inform organisations in a supportive manner. It draws on many years of experience that include dealing with the most sensitive types of intelligence.

In 2019 he published a critically acclaimed non-fiction guide to speaking up 'Exposing the Truth – Whistleblowing Uncovered'.

'Jeopardy' is his second book. It has been written with a background and a great deal of experience in the specialist and dangerous world of informant handling. The book explores current issues that are affecting policing in the 21st century and gives a rare first-hand insight into a work environment that very few experience.

iTrust Assurance Limited offers a comprehensive range of whistle-blower-related services.

Nick welcomes questions and comments from readers. You can contact him via the iTrust Assurance Limited website www. itrustassuarance.co.uk and via Twitter @itrustassure.

Chapter 1

Detective Inspector Jim Fowler was being rapidly promoted through the ranks. He was 42 years old. He had previously served in the Royal Military Police for seven years and had reached the rank of Corporal, but being ambitious, couldn't see where his career with the Army was heading. He'd had enough of the uncertainty of public sector cutbacks and had wanted a more settled life; a family life. He liked policing and decided a career in a provincial police force would suit him just fine. Before he knew it he had resigned from the Army and joined Dorshire Police. It had been a whirlwind few months and in what seemed like no time at all was walking the beat in Padmouth. Padmouth was a typical tired, rundown British seaside town which had seen better days. However, it boasted a small marina and had aspirations to go upmarket, but in typical British seaside fashion still had a very long way to go.

Padmouth was not what he had been expecting for his first posting, and it couldn't have been further removed from what he had been used to. At exactly the same point twelve months earlier and in complete contrast, he had been skiing with the Army amongst snow-capped mountains in southern Germany. That was really enjoyable and not what the average person would call hard work. Yet despite being a windy, rainy night walking the beat on Padmouth seafront, Jim knew he had made the right decision.

He was a quiet man, not one for many friends or wild nights out. Intelligent, determined and resolute, confident in his own abilities, tall and athletic, a man of few words - and with ambition. He knew that a windy, rainy night in Padmouth would not be the pinnacle of his career.

Jim loved being a copper. When he joined Dorshire Police he quickly became part of a close-knit team. It was the sort of comradery he had enjoyed in the Army which made for an easier transition from one uniform seamlessly into another. From being a uniformed constable policing Padmouth he quickly moved into the Criminal Investigative Division (CID). This is where he honed his investigative skills. He was far better suited to this type of environment. It was less confrontational than a uniformed role and it gave him time to think; for Jim was a thinker, and he was ruthless. He went for the jugular and frequently got suspects to admit their offence. As an ace detective he shone in CID and was quickly supported for promotion, so after only three years in the force became a Sergeant. A short stint back in uniform followed from where he then went into Public Protection, managing a team who dealt with victims of domestic abuse. This was not what he really liked but having stuck it out for two years he transferred to Major Crime. Jim loved it there, cementing a reputation for having a no-nonsense approach to policing. His aspirations grew and he passed the next promotion exam; he was then elevated to the rank of Inspector.

He spent just over a year back in uniform, but his career and ambition lay elsewhere. He had never been part of the world of covert policing and desperately wanted to get involved. To him it just seemed a more effective way of catching criminals and he needed the experience for his promotion portfolio, but this was a time of financial restraint and cutbacks. The world of covert policing was shrinking along with the rest of the policing world. There were very few opportunities, especially for officers with rank. In his no-nonsense way, Jim told the senior ranks what he thought about the cutbacks and where they *should* be made, not where they were *being* made. His style of management had also been commented on by one of his team as oppressive, during what Dorshire Police called a '360' appraisal' – where staff could anonymously appraise their managers. He had a reputation for getting the job done, but in the process was considered as being a rather confrontational and somewhat abrasive character. Instead of learning from it, Jim had tried to find out who had said he was oppressive, and this hadn't been well received by his supervisors or those he supervised.

He didn't take well to criticism, but the policing world was rapidly changing and Jim hadn't really moved with the times. This was not a good step in the very political world of police management and before he knew it he was placed on a project – at the Home Office. This was the policing equivalent of being put on the 'naughty step'; long hours, boring work and a lengthy commute into London and back every day. For some this setback could have been the end of a career, but an opportunity arose on a neighbourhood unit as a Detective Inspector (DI) with a return to Padmouth. Jim jumped at the chance. A job back in the force, and the prospect of resurrecting his career.

The neighbourhood unit was not just any neighbourhood unit.

It was a flagship project, funded by the Home Office. It wasn't the most glamorous of postings but one where Jim could use his limited but established networks. Jim had worked with some of those who had been responsible for its conception, so knew exactly what was wanted and how to deliver it. It was ideal; a perfect fit, a chance for him to showcase his skills. A straight-forward project to demonstrate how he could blend the personalities of the different agencies who had to come together to improve the lives of those living in a socially deprived area of the county, let alone the country. This was a new challenge with the police as the lead agency, and more importantly a chance for him to establish himself as a DI and take the next step towards becoming a Detective Chief Inspector (DCI).

The 'Padmouth Task Force', as it became known, soon established itself as the benchmark by which other projects would be graded in the country. It was a public relations success and Jim shone. Regular visits by those in government from London to the coast ensured that Jim's stock was increasing again - and his bosses loved it. Innovation in a time of cutbacks was just what was needed. Dorshire Police was once again leading the way across the country by showing what was possible in a climate of reducing budgets, and the public demanding more from less. A multi-agency community initiative that had a direct benefit for those that it served; a public-relations triumph.

Jim had felt settled once again and was liked by his team. There were those whom he had known from his early days in Padmouth who he could trust to get the job done. They were a tight-knit bunch, and mates from the days when he was a Police Constable (PC).

They had a great team spirit and it was very much how policing used to be – work hard, play hard. They covered each other's backs at work and off duty too. They socialised with each other, which helped build a comradery that Jim enjoyed and encouraged. There were regular after-work drinks and the occasional party in a section house, which is how they got to know each other better. This hadn't gone down well at home between Jim and his wife Lorraine, but Jim knew that he had to do it to make the team a success. Good times were aplenty and Jim enjoyed himself with the team more than for a long time in his career. Jim knew his team well and his mates inside out. He knew how they operated.

One, PC Dave Harrison, had a military background like him and they got on particularly well. Dave was from Padmouth and had grown up in the town. He had left school at 16 to join The Royal Artillery, but had gotten disillusioned after a few years and then joined Dorshire Police. He knew where everything was and knew most of the people too ; he could get things sorted. Dave was one of those PCs of whom you did not ask any questions when it came to getting things done. He was a loner, a bit like Jim, and he too did not like being challenged. He would either ignore difficult questions, or aggressively come back at those who dared question him. It was therefore easier to ignore him. He was protected by Jim, and maybe it was because of the military connection or just being similar in character but that was just the way it was. Some on the team flew closer to the wind than others but if they did their job, Jim didn't mind.

PC Pete Solomon was another ex-military type who Jim got on with very well but left a short time after Jim started on the team, as he retired due to ill health. It was a time when ill health retirements were commonplace, a way of getting a pension through the back door. It was another example of how the task force held on to an old-school way of policing from a bygone era. If the job got done, that was what it was all about - no messing. For Jim it was all about making the team a success and making sure he re-established his reputation. New colleagues from other agencies all wanted to see the new team succeed too, oblivious to Jim and his team's ways. The team was heralded as great success. Accolade after accolade followed.

But Jim was still missing something. He needed the tick-in-the-box of covert policing to get to that next rank. Jim had never really understood covert policing. It was all the work of the dark arts - of surveillance, cameras, bugs and spies. He had never seen the worth of all the time and expense that went into the management of the covert side of the business. Informants were what police 'used' in the bad old days. A snitch who would tip them off in return for bail or even no charge at all. Jim was very much a champion of uniformed police and good old-fashioned detective work.

Jim had a plan. To gain promotion he would be able to successfully argue the case for reducing the number of informants in Dorshire Police, and thus reduce the budget in that department. He knew how to obtain results, and this next chapter in his career would be no different. But first he had to get to know how the informant system worked, to then be able to fight his corner in reducing the expense of running the team. All he had to do was convince his boss, the Head of the Serious Crime Department, Assistant Chief Constable (ACC) Rick Donning, that his plans were sound and promotion would be his.

Dan Ellis was also a DI. He was more experienced than Jim and had been a Controller at CO15 for six years. He was used to the world of covert policing and managing informants. He had seen the lot; from informants who had provided information about low-level criminality, to those reporting about terrorism and corruption. It wasn't a pretty world. Double crossing and fabrication - and then there were the informants. Dan could see the future, with even more cutbacks. This was not what he wanted, and he wanted out; he was off to pastures new. There were no other takers for the job and Jim saw his opportunity. This was his moment. He knew that if he could make cuts to the team, then that could be his ticket to the next rank. After all, it was all about saving money in the current climate and his bosses would love him if he could achieve that. He had a track record of going for the jugular and he figured this could work here too. He had nineteen and a half years' service and he reckoned he could achieve a few more ranks before he finished his career.

Chapter 2

Jim sat at his desk. It had been a long week. He was tired and didn't fancy going out for a leaving drink. He just wanted to go home, but he knew he had to go and see DI Dan Ellis off - it was his duty. Besides, Dan had been in post for a few years - it was only right and proper that he went along. Jim had just taken over from Dan and he was now the new Controller at CO15. CO15 was the most prestigious informant handling team in Dorshire Police and was part of the covert operations department. The position of Controller was a good job - especially if you wanted promotion. Not everyone wanted it, as it came with a lot of stress and very little thanks, but plenty of criticism if it went wrong. A job where you had to think on your feet but took no glory. It involved managing informants who gave intelligence of the riskier type – about firearms, large-scale drug supply, armed robberies and the occasional bit of work involving police corruption. It was not a job for the faint-hearted.

Dan and Jim didn't really get on, but going out for Dan's leaving drink was just the right thing to do. There would be others in the pub Jim knew and that would take the edge off it he thought. He didn't have to stay for long, just show a face to placate the senior ranks and toe the social line.

Jim had only been in the job for a couple of weeks and was still finding his feet. He had been given a bit of a handover from Dan but not much of one. This was typical of Dorshire Police. The organisation putting people into a job and then training them how to do it. However, Jim was a confident supervisor. He carried an air of authority, and had been schooled to become 'a presence in the room' by one his promotion mentors. He liked being 'a presence' as he had learnt it meant there were then fewer challenges to his decisions. This was the old-school way of thinking that he valued.

Jim looked at his watch. It was 6.22pm. He knew he had to go to the pub, not only to support his colleague but also for his own sanity. He had been working very long hours. It wasn't just the everyday work that he had to deal with, it was the extra projects he'd been given to 'aid' his development in becoming a DCI. This was the police all over. As soon as you put your head above the parapet and said you were even *thinking* about promotion, the extra work came piling in. It was just an extra pressure he didn't need. Jim knew this would happen and he was at a rank that was not a great one in which to be stuck. As a DI he was pressured from the ranks above and pressured from the ranks below. Even as a DCI he knew he wouldn't earn much more pay than being a DI, but knew like everyone else who had gone before him it was a stepping-stone to becoming a Superintendent. This would be a rank with more money, a larger pension, certainly more prestige, *and* a way of getting to the next rank of Chief Superintendent before he retired. If he didn't get the substantive Chief Superintendent rank, he may be able to pull a few strings and secure a temporary promotion which would help boost his pension.

Jim was a family man with two teenage daughters and a loving wife. They were a quiet couple who didn't have a wide circle of friends. They liked gardening and the routine of yearly foreign holidays many suburban families enjoy. Jim had met his wife Lorraine whilst they had been at police training college together but hadn't got together until he moved into CID. Jim tutored Lorraine when she was training to become a detective but once there became an item. Unfortunately for them, their supervisors thought it best to ensure they worked on different teams and since that time, despite both serving in the police for nearly 20 years, their professional paths had not crossed, excepting when he tutored her. This suited them as she became pregnant soon after they met and needed to make the shifts work so they could spend time as a family. Lorraine was happy for Jim to pursue his professional career whilst she remained a detective in a vulnerable victim's role. In fact if she could have done, she would have left the job a few years earlier; it was not what she'd envisaged and was keen to leave. Pension changes, the lack of support from the public as well as from certain managers in the force had all taken their toll. Lorraine had suffered as a result. She had found it a struggle to cope with the stresses and strains of modern-day policing and had sought professional help. Jim was sympathetic to a point but not much of a help. Maybe it was because of his military background and stoic angle on life. But he loved his wife and it worked.

Jim tidied his desk and turned off his computer. He closed the window blind and picked up his briefcase. He pushed his chair under his desk and checked that his desk was tidy. He straightened the picture of Lorraine – it was a picture of them embracing in a restaurant whilst on holiday in Spain the year before — and walked towards the door of his office. He glanced at his bookcase. He noticed the framed certificates which he'd lined up at the back of the second shelf down; he was most proud of his Certificate in Terrorism Studies. He'd passed the course nearly three years ago and this had undoubtedly helped him to gain promotion. The top brass liked officers to do extra things to show commitment to the cause. His family had been so proud of him at the ceremony at Headquarters when he was presented with the certificate by a Home Office minister. As he left his office, he pulled the door closed. He walked purposefully through the open-plan office where his team had been working that day and walked towards the main door. The office was neat and tidy – the way he liked it. Everyone in the office had left just after 4pm and gone to the pub for Dan's leaving drink. Jim knew that most were driving so it wouldn't be too rowdy. He was looking forward to a couple of pints. He had arranged for Lorraine to pick him up so he could relax a bit; God, he needed it. She would be there about 8-8:30pm, so he had a bit of time. As he left the main office he turned out the lights, set the alarm and went down the stairs. His swipe card beeped as he let himself out of the building.

The cold January air hit him as he walked past a police car being washed by a young officer. The officer looked up from scrubbing the rear bumper of the car. "Evenin' guv." "Evenin'," Jim replied in his harsh Scottish accent. His accent meant that on occasion he was difficult to understand. He headed towards the gate at the rear of Dorshire Police Headquarters. He took his phone out of his coat pocket and as he walked he texted Lorraine. "Just finished. In pub. See you at 8.30". He looked up. He could see the sign – 'The Punch and Judy' — hanging over the entrance to the pub. Known as The Punch, it had seen many a 'leaving do', some better attended than others.

It was a Friday evening so he knew the pub would be packed. He could hear the noise from inside it as he got nearer and saw a couple of blokes smoking outside the front door. He nodded to the two fellas as if to acknowledge them as he walked into the pub's narrow entrance. He pulled open a door to let himself into its main room. As he did so a wall of noise greeted him. What a din. It was the usual Friday night scene but even more packed that evening. He could see his team along with others he knew at the end of the bar, and he gradually made his way through the throng of people to get to them. Over the noise Jim heard "What do you want, guv? I'll get you one." "Lager please. Cheers." Martin was Jim's Sergeant. He was a cheery soul and always good for a laugh. He had been a Sergeant on the team for three years and had worked in every role in the world of informant management across the force for 15 years. He had worked both as an informant handler and as a supervisor for Special Branch. This included working with MI5. There wasn't much that he hadn't done or seen when it came to managing informants. He had a bit more service than Jim but had never previously worked with him. They were poles apart in terms of personality, but Martin was ever the optimist, and had always worked with his previous bosses to ensure the team they managed together consistently produced the best results.

"I didn't think you would get here, guv," said Martin. "Missing in action?" Jim smiled. "Just finishing off the report for the ACC. The

Surveillance Commissioner comes to inspect us in three weeks' time and she wants to know what the top results have been this year." "Oh," replied Martin. But the noise was so great that the two of them were struggling to make themselves heard. They sipped their beers and Martin nodded. There wasn't too much point in trying to make conversation. He was a chatty soul but even he didn't think there was much point in trying any harder to get a conversation out of Jim.

There were no senior ranks left that Jim could see in the pub. Maybe they had just had the one drink at the end of work and then made their excuses. Jim was a man of few words and Martin had plenty to say about a lot of things. But this was not the place for anyone to try and make a sensible conversation about anything really. Jim could see Dan and went over to chat to him. "So when do you start proper?" said Jim. Dan replied, "Monday in earnest. You know it'll take a few weeks to settle in and find my feet, then I'll start making a few changes. If there is anything you need Jim, just let me know; it's a difficult job running 60-something snouts across the county. You need to keep your wits about you - and that's just the Source Handlers. They'll try and have you over if you're not on it." Jim smiled. "Thanks Dan. I'll be okay." They were both very conscious not to speak too openly due to the sensitive nature of their business and had become aware that the pub had become a little quieter. A group of lads who had been standing in one corner of the room had just left so there was a bit more room. They were local lads and had met up at The Punch for their first drink before heading off into town. A bit of breathing space and a chance to hear yourself think, Jim thought.

Michelle and Andy were standing next to Jim and Dan. "Did you like your man-bag, Sir?" Michelle asked Dan. He had been bought it as a leaving present by the department. "Yes, Michelle, very nice, thanks. I'll think of you all when I'm on my way to my very important meetings," Dan laughed. The group all joined in. Others came up to Dan and were chatting and everyone was getting on. Jim finished his pint. He looked at his phone. No calls or texts. It was 7.54pm. Time for a quick one. He was aware that there was a whip but hadn't put into it. "Dan. Can I get you a drink?" "No thanks. I've just got this — cheers," he said. Jim went to the bar and got himself another lager and went back to where the group were standing. He was starving, he hadn't eaten since lunchtime. He could see a few sandwiches were left as Dan had ordered a buffet for his leaving do. Jim picked them up and was grateful just to get some food inside him. He ended up chatting to people in his team about work and the future of the department, about the police and how it had changed during his time in the job.

He checked his phone again as he was conscious time was getting on; it was 8.28pm. Lorraine would be here soon so he put his drink down and went to the toilet. It was up a couple of steps and right at the back of the pub. He opened the door to the gents and went into the toilet. Standing next to him at the urinal he became aware of someone washing their hands. "You okay boss?" said a voice in a slurred Irish accent. Jim looked round. "Oh. You. You pissed up bastard." Paul carried on washing his hands. Even with Jim's limited ability at making conversation he knew that there was no point in trying to make conversation with Paul. They had known each other a long time having been on the same uniformed section together in Padmouth, and their professional paths had crossed several times during their careers. They were cut from the same cloth and had a respect for each other. In fact it went beyond that, and over the years they had regularly maintained contact, albeit they didn't socialise together. Paul Slacke was a uniformed Sergeant and was just the sort of officer Jim wanted to work with again, but he too had no covert policing experience. Jim knew he would find it difficult to get him into his team. Paul was also based at Headquarters but on a traffic process unit. This team sorted out the administration of speeding tickets and fixed penalty notices for motoring offences. In terms of personnel he was responsible for managing a small team of civilians but as such had no police officers to supervise. Paul preferred this, as police officers were inevitably more difficult to manage, although he'd been in the unit for only a couple of years. Paul was ex-military and had the sort of mentality that Jim liked and understood.

Jim knew it was difficult to have a conversation with Paul at the best of times and thought it was just easier to ignore him on this occasion. He also knew he wouldn't be able to get a drink out of Paul as he wasn't the most generous of mates, even when he'd had a few too many to drink. As Paul left the toilet Jim said "Look after yourself, catch up next week," and the door closed. Jim washed his hands, held them under the drier for a few moments and exited the toilet.

As he walked down the length of the pub back to where he had been standing he could see that Lorraine had come into the pub to collect him. She was standing with his team. He checked his phone. "Here, darling. Don't rush. I'll park up and pop in". She never normally came in to get him. "Can I get you a drink?" he said. "Just a ... lemonade, please, darling," she said. Jim went to the bar and ordered a lemonade and another lager. He took the drinks back to Lorraine where the others were standing and joined in the conversation.

By this time the pub was a lot quieter than it had been earlier in the evening and some of his team had gone home. Lorraine was chatting to Michelle, Martin and Andy. She knew Michelle and Martin, having been on a CID course with them earlier in her career. Jim was listening but not really saying much. Lorraine seemed to be enjoying herself. Martin was his usual chatty self and making everyone laugh, the life and soul. Andy was a bit more reserved and Michelle chipped in with the odd quip. The conversation revolved around holidays, where everyone was planning to go in the next few months - and what everyone was having to eat that night once they had left the pub. Nothing of any great note. Jim was feeling a bit left out. He just wanted to get home as he was bored and tired. He interrupted. "Come on, Lorraine. Let's go". Lorraine was enjoying herself but knew that Jim was getting fed up. "Oh, okay, got to go. Nice to see you all again," she said. Lorraine leaned forward and gave everyone a peck on the cheek. Dan acknowledged them both by nodding as Jim and Lorraine left the pub. "All the best," said Jim. He looked towards his team. "And don't you lot get into any mischief. I don't want to have to be dealing with any disciplinaries on Monday morning!". With that, he left the pub.

You could feel the atmosphere lift as Jim left the pub. In the short time that he had been managing the CO15 tcam they had quickly regarded him as being a miserable sod and hadn't really taken to him as a boss. They decided they knew what he was all about and that he'd taken this job to get promoted. He had no experience in covert policing and he took no advice from either them or his predecessor Dan. They had heard rumours about his ways whilst he was on the Padmouth Task Force but hadn't realised how miserable and aggressive he was and turning out to be. They thought he had been promoted well above his ability. This had been proven over the last couple of weeks as he acted without taking advice from anyone.

Jim knew that he wasn't well liked but didn't really care. It was all about him, and getting a tick in the box for promotion. But the team was professional and went about their work in the way they had done for years. They were a team of very experienced informant handlers and there wasn't much they hadn't seen. "Never trust a man who tucks his shirt into his pants," said Martin. "Ruddy miserable idiot." Michelle and Andy laughed. "I hope he has a crap weekend. Poor Lorraine; I don't know what she sees in him. Love is blind and all that." Michelle agreed. "Jeopardy Jim!" she announced. Jim had used the word "jeopardy" a lot during the two weeks he had been their boss and the team had quickly given him the title of 'Jeopardy Jim'. Everyone laughed. Jim had only been managing the team a short time, but had already got a reputation for being risk averse. He wasn't used to managing informants and all that came with it. Like making a life and death decision based on a call from an informant in the middle of the night. It was not a role quite like anything he had experienced in his career before. Hence, he used the term jeopardy quite a lot in his repertoire.

It was a cold, crisp evening and getting colder by the hour. A frost was forming on the parked cars next to the pavement as Jim and

Lorraine walked the short distance towards their car. Jim rema__ silent. The atmosphere was dark like the clear night sky. Lorraine tried to make conversation. "Nice to see them again," she said. Jim said nothing. "That Martin looks well. He is always upbeat and smiling and Michelle always looks happy. I don't know Andy, but he seems nice, too." Jim said nothing. "Wish we could have stayed a bit longer. You've got a nice team. There are a few more I think that weren't there, but..." Jim cut her short. "Shut up! They're a jumped-up bunch and lucky to have their jobs. Been there too long. Martin loves himself. Michelle thinks she's God's gift and Andy does what he is told by Michelle. The others can't be arsed to come out."

"Jim. That's a bit harsh," Lorraine replied. "They're nice. Just because you're . . . " Jim cut her short again.

"What? You fancy Andy or Martin or something?"

"Jim!" What's *up* with you?" She knew that he'd had a few drinks and thought better than to argue with him. It was always Jim's way of trying to stop her from going out and socialising. She knew he had a way of controlling her but she went along with him just to keep the peace. He had always been jealous of any male company she had ever kept no matter how minimal, and the drink always exaggerated his personality.

After a few more minutes they had reached Lorraine's car, and drove home which took about twenty minutes. As Lorraine was driving, the silence was deafening. Then she cautiously said in a hushed tone. "Martin seems to like you. He is quite funny. He must be quite popular on the team." He cut her short again, suddenly turning towards her and raising his right hand along with his voice. "*Shut* it, Lorraine!" he shouted. "Any more behaviour like I've seen tonight and you'll see the back of my hand again." Lorraine knew exactly what he meant. He had hit her several times across her face during their marriage but hadn't done so for several years. She had previously put it down to stress at work, and although she knew what he'd done obviously wasn't right, she could never bring herself to report him. She was extremely loyal to Jim and didn't want him to lose his career. They had built a comfortable life together and she didn't want to let it go. She feared Jim but was even more scared of the repercussions if she left him. The car fell quiet.

A short while later they arrived home. Still nothing more was said. Lorraine had seen Jim in this sort of state before, as he didn't cope well with pressure as well as being tired. This was combined with a few drinks on an empty stomach after a long week so she hoped he'd be in a better mood the next day. Tomorrow would always be a better day, she thought.

Chapter 3

"Morning, Michelle!" Martin cheerily quipped as she came through the door to the office. "Morning," she replied in her soft Geordie accent. Michelle was slightly late for work today but that was because one of her sons forgot to pack his PE kit and she had to help him find it before school. She was usually very organised and was still annoyed about her son's lack in this area. A typical 15-year-old, she thought. Michelle had another son who was 13 years old. She was married to an ex-copper who was now a civilian working on a surveillance team. She was well used to living the life of a covert officer and all that it involved. Michelle had been a nurse before she had joined Dorshire Police and longed to get back to a caring role. She had a big heart and was considered the mothering soul on the team. She hadn't long until she retired but was one of life's grafters. She loved her job and was very good at it. There wasn't much she hadn't seen or done in her time and could talk the hind leg off a donkey; and she did things right. There was no place in Michelle's world for taking any shortcuts and she didn't suffer fools. What she thought she said, and this had upset Jim; the two didn't get on as she'd told him a few home truths.

It wasn't normal for her to be late for work. It had been another weekend of taking calls from informants and Martin and Michelle had taken the brunt of the information they had provided. It all needed to be recorded, assessed and disseminated. Martin and Michelle hadn't seen each other since Friday evening at the pub but it was as if they had worked together all weekend. Michelle's phone hadn't stopped ringing and she had to phone Martin afterwards. The life of an informant handler or their supervisor never stopped. The information kept coming in day and night and didn't stop for weekends; this had been just one of those weekends. "Everything alright?" Martin asked. "No, not really," said Michelle. "Too much like bloody grief. If it's not someone trying to kill someone again, it's our colleagues not doing anything with the information. There's no one left to work on it. I don't feel like I've had a break from it either over the weekend. And what for?" Josh and Andy were in the office too. They were busying themselves for the day and week ahead. Josh piped up, "You're pretty busy now, Michelle. If there's anything you need me to do, just ask". "No, pet," Michelle said. "Very kind."

Martin was 48 years old and married with two teenage children. He was a happy soul, always positive and upbeat. He had an optimistic view of life, a great quality to have in his role, as all day his life revolved around dealing with information that involved high-level criminality. It seemed like the whole world was continually committing crime. He had six years to go before he retired and had no intention of seeking promotion. He had seen what had happened to most of those who had and vowed not to allow it to happen to him. He had also seen some of those promoted as being completely useless at supervising, and although he hadn't worked with Jim for very long he was having serious doubts about him and his leadership abilities.

Josh was 34 years old and was the youngest in the team. He was married with a two-year old son. He had only been in the team for three and a half years but was an excellent informant handler. He was studying for promotion and had ambitions to become a Sergeant. He had been in the police for nine years but had a knack of being able to put people quickly at ease, and hence had found his way into the world of informant management a short time into his career. He was a personal trainer before he joined the police as well as a martial arts expert. This was a great quality to have as an informant handler.

Andy had been in the office for over ten years and was the voice of experience. He was 45 years old, had a partner but had never married. They had two grown-up children. He was one of life's nice blokes. Someone you would want as a neighbour who would do anything for you, one who was always there and who could be relied on to give great advice. He was solid and dependable. Andy and Michelle had been on the team for about the same amount of time; it was a good blend.

Several years before the team had been greater in terms of numbers, but were now down to four informant handlers because Louise had recently been promoted. The CO15 team were a close-knit bunch - they had to be because of the volume of work they had as well as the pressure of their role. Managing numerous high-risk informants was no easy feat. It had taken a toll on their mental health over the years, constantly being on call, and waiting for the phone to ring at any time 24 hours a day, seven days a week. When the team was much larger and they had more informants to manage, the workload was that much more extensive and there was less scrutiny about their working practices, but over the years the team had become more professional and skilled. However, prior to this, their work had included taking calls when they were on holiday, such was their dedication to the role. This had changed slightly but the stress remained. Up until a few years before they had been given yearly psychological checks, but with the advent of austerity these had gone. They relied heavily on the support of their colleagues and being able to speak freely at work about their feelings. Some were better than others, particularly Michelle who frequently didn't hold back, not only with Jim but occasionally she rubbed the rest of the team up the wrong way as well. But they were a forgiving team, and like any family tolerated each other at the same time as being the closest of teams; they just had to be. They had been reduced to the bare minimum over the last few years due to budget cuts, and they had fought their corner to stop any further loss in manpower. Their results proved their worth and despite being a covert team they'd achieved notable successes. It was tough being in this particular crew, let alone continually looking over their collective shoulders to see if they were destined for the next round of cuts. They knew their worth and the value of informants, and were determined to fight to save their jobs. If need be, they would go down fighting.

Everyone was at their desks checking e-mails and diaries. "Right. Everyone ready for the meeting?" The daily briefing was a chance for them all to catch up, to learn about what everyone had on for the day and for Martin to deal with any general administration issues needing to be addressed. "Good morning. Hope everyone is well and had a good weekend – apart from you, Michelle, obviously." Wry smiles from everyone. "So what have you got on today, Michelle?" "Catch up from the weekend and do a shed load of typing I suppose," she said. "I've got to put a call into Ambrose Wilks and see if he's up for a meeting tomorrow. I've got 200 quid for him." "Anything else?" asked Martin. "Nope," came the reply. Michelle was usually quite chatty, but she was tired. It had been a long weekend. "Josh. What you got on?" queried Martin. "I'm meeting Kayne Woolery today at 11 with Andy," Josh answered. "If you could do the cover please, that would be good." "Sorry," Martin responded. "Tasking Group Meeting." This was the pattern of how it had gone recently. Too many cuts, not enough staff, increasing demands but the same number of meetings. Josh grinned. He was resigned to this as it had become the norm. "Andy. What have you got on?"

At this point the office door opened and Jim walked in. "Mornin'." "Morning, Sir," said Martin. Jim walked through the centre of the office and sat down at his desk in an annex in the far corner of the main office; it looked like he wasn't in a good mood. He'd had a busy weekend taking calls from all over the county. But although this was the job, he hadn't expected it to be like this. This is not how Dan had described it . A lot of thinking, yes, but not non-stop call-taking. He could hear Martin finishing off the briefing. "Sorry, Andy," Martin went on. "What have you got on today?" "I'm going out with Josh to meet Kayne and I need to put a call in to Lee Heavney; he left a message on Saturday asking me to call this afternoon. He's due to move prison soon and I need to speak to him to see where he thinks he's going and if there are any issues to sort out." Jim overheard this. He raised his voice as he spoke to Andy from his annex. "Andy — when you speak to him tell him he's sacked. He's not giving us enough information and he's carrying too much jeopardy. He can have the money he's owed but he's not getting any more after that." Andy had thought this might be coming. "Okay boss." Lee Heavney had been a decent informant but had gone off the boil in the last month. But that was the way it was sometimes with informants in prison. They had access to great information but then it usually dried up. And that was why Heavney wanted to be moved – to start getting more information. He had been particularly good at obtaining details about corrupt prison officers and one in particular — but that only had a certain shelf-life. Andy knew that although Jim was cancelling Heavney's informant authority he would phone in once he had moved prison and start producing good quality intelligence again. Andy looked at Martin and raised his eyebrows. Nothing Jim did surprised him; he was risk averse and didn't like informants in prison. Martin thought that this would be a good time to close the meeting. "Well, have a good day everyone and make sure the cars are clean. At this time of year in particular the cars get dirty really quickly. And make sure that they are tidy please. No one wants to sit in anyone else's mess, thank you! Oh...and the VW Golf needs fuel, please." Andy smiled. Martin was a stickler for tidiness and although it sometimes got beyond a joke he knew it was just Martin maintaining standards. The two cars they used on the team were unmarked vehicles and had normal-looking number plates, but were registered under the team's covert business. They had to be, so the whole record of the team could withstand scrutiny if challenged. No one wanted to be seen with an informant handler so everyone on the team worked in plain clothes. It was a nice blend of two males and two females on the team, so any cover story they employed worked perfectly. It was a sort of mix-and-match system, but invariably Andy and Josh paired up together and Michelle and Helen likewise.

Michelle was hungry and wanted some breakfast. She had arrived late for work because of her son's inability to organise himself on a Sunday night and needed to refuel. "Who fancies some breakfast?" she said to the office. At that point both Helen and Ellie came through the office doors in a rush. "Sorry I'm late, Martin. The motorway was just awful, Monday mornings are getting worse and the traffic was a nightmare today" Ellie apologised too. "Me too, Martin. We should really lift-share but with the kids, you know how it is if we have to get off early." "Yes, yes," Martin said. Helen and Ellie went and sat down at their desks.

Helen was a 37-year old mum with twin daughters who were at pre school. Her husband was a copper too so they both appreciated what each other did at work and what responsibilities they each had. Every day was a rush for Helen. She had worked for Dorshire Police for four years as a civilian and then joined up as a constable. She loved her work and had been an informant handler for just a little longer than Josh. The hours suited Helen and she was 100% sure that she wanted to stay in this role if she could. Going to a role in uniform would not be conducive to a healthy marriage, as she had witnessed during her time with the police.

Ellie was 23 years old and was very competent as an Administrative Researcher, researching and collating the information informants gave the handlers, and disseminating it to whoever needed to read it; nothing was too much trouble for her. Her husband was also a copper, so like Helen she knew what the job was all about. Ellie was the quiet one in the office, just getting her head down and going about her job with a calm efficiency.

Michelle said again, "Helen and Ellie. I just asked whether anyone wanted to get some breakfast in the canteen?" Before either of them could reply a voice boomed from the corner of the office. "Not today, guys. There's a lot to do and you haven't got the time. I know you have only just sat down, Ellie, but can you get last month's stats to me by 10.15? Thanks." Jim had extinguished any enthusiasm the team had been having for the day, as well as the week ahead. This was a skill Jim possessed in abundance and doing so was becoming a trend. The trend was on an upward path, and had become worse in the two weeks since Jim had taken over the role from Dan. There was no real reason why. The team had discussed the situation, and agreed that it was him stamping his authority to make sure they knew it was *he* who was in charge.

There were knowing looks all around the office as the team resigned themselves to not having breakfast at that particular time - but they all knew they would just go out when Jim had disappeared to a meeting, which he did on Mondays at 11.00 am, and have it then. Who was *he* to tell them they couldn't eat?

Everyone got their heads down and started work at their computers. There were records of contacts with informants to type, e-mails to check and general admin tasks to catch up on that had come in over the weekend. There wasn't much of a conversation going on in the office. A cloud had descended since Jim had come into work and it wasn't what they were used to, or enjoyed.

It wasn't long before the silence was broken. "The stats are done and in your pot, boss," said Ellie. "Cheers, Ellie," said Jim. An hour passed, and Jim stood up from his desk. "Right. See you all later. I'm off to the 10.30 meeting." "See you later, guvnor," said Martin. Although he wasn't Jim's biggest fan he was loyal and made sure the job was done properly. He didn't have the same outlook on life as Jim, but realised it takes all sorts and told himself Jim was just a different type of supervisor.

As soon as Jim disappeared from the office the team started talking. "What a kill-joy!" said Andy. "He's getting bloody worse. What's up with him?" Josh chipped in: "I knew he was a miserable sod before he started here, but..." As Josh was about to carry on talking there was a knock at the door. Michelle's desk was closest to the door and because of this she got up and opened it. It was Sergeant Paul Slacke. He was standing just outside the door, looking officious in his uniform. He was there for the 10.30am meeting, too. "Is he in?" Paul asked in his clipped Irish accent. He was out of breath having just climbed two flights of stairs to reach the office. Paul was considered mentally unstable by his own team of civilians and more generally by anyone who had ever worked with him in his 29-year career. He was nearing retirement and was counting down the days to the finishing line. In fact, he had been counting them down for not far short of 29 years - so had his colleagues and former colleagues; he wasn't well-liked. He was ex-Army and had a found a kindred spirit in Jim; they were cut from the same cloth. Both had chequered police careers, but somehow managed to become elevated to middle management in Dorshire Police. Paul was a short podgy man with a gut, testament to the pints of beer he consumed virtually every night and possibly even with breakfast.

On some days his own team had suspected he smelled of booze at his desk. He had an unpredictable character and a very short fuse; everyone was too fearful of challenging him. Those who did got short shrift, so everybody else subsequently didn't bother. Paul couldn't live with his partner Mandy, as she would not and could not tolerate his drinking and ensuing abusive behaviour. His reputation was not great, but he'd had a charmed existence within the force.

As he stood at the door, Michelle was taken aback by the overpowering stench of cheap aftershave, and thought she could smell the whiff of stale alcohol on his breath; however, she thought better than to mention it to him. It would have got her in trouble with him as well as Jim, if he then told him. "You've just missed him, Sarge," said Michelle. "He's gone to the 10.30 meeting." "Okay, no problem," Paul replied and quickly hurried off to find him. Martin's team knew Jim and Paul had worked together years ago, and during the last two weeks had got used to Paul appearing at the office door waiting to go for a coffee or to another meeting. The team suspected that the meetings were just a cover for yet another coffee and gossip.

"Right, everyone. Five minutes and I'm off to get breakfast. Anyone coming?" called Michelle. There was a resounding "yes" from everyone and soon after they all traipsed out of the office to the canteen. The team made the short walk down the creaky stairs to the canteen and queued for their breakfast. The smell of mass-produced, greasy breakfasts wafted through the canteen. The room was busy with an assortment of ranks. The Deputy Chief

Constable was sitting with his three Assistant Chief Constables at the table reserved for them. People chatted noisily as they caught up after the weekend. Not many people worked weekends if they were based in a headquarters role and there was plenty of catching up to do. As they waited patiently, Jim's wife Lorraine wandered in with a colleague and joined the back of the queue. "Hi guys," she said, having recognised some of them from the pub the previous Friday. "Hi Lorraine," answered Michelle. She was a bit more upbeat as she was nearing the point of silencing her pangs of hunger. "How are you?" "All good, thanks," said Lorraine cheerily. "I'm on a refresher course. You've gotta love headquarters — you've got a canteen!" The team laughed. Lorraine wasn't based at Headquarters and a trip there was a novelty. "Come and join us for breakfast," said Michelle. "That'd be lovely. I'll join you in a minute," she said.

Once they'd placed their orders, they sat at one big table making small talk about nothing in particular. Lorraine asked Martin about his next holiday and what his plans were. "Vietnam next year with the family, but before that..." At that moment Jim appeared at the door to the canteen with Paul Slacke. The 10.30am meeting had been postponed by an hour due to the heavy traffic on the motorway which had delayed people getting to Headquarters, so they had decided to go the canteen for a coffee. They were in deep in conversation but stopped abruptly in their tracks when they saw who was in the canteen. Jim looked and glared at the group, including his wife, who had stopped chatting. The team knew there was going to be trouble. Jim continued to glare at the whole team as well as Lorraine, who was seated opposite Martin. Jim knew he couldn't say anything there and then as the room was even more packed as people who had piled in for breakfast. But the team had the feeling their week was about to get a whole lot worse.

Chapter 4

Josh and Andy were on the way to the meeting with Kayne Woolery; their mood was subdued. They were in the team's unmarked VW Golf. The car was dark grey, just like their week had suddenly become. "What did you make of all that?" said Josh. "At breakfast?" Andy asked. "Yes. What was the boss like? Do you think he checked up on us on purpose?" said Josh. "Of course, he just doesn't trust us. I think Martin is going to cop it as he could have told us not to go to breakfast but allowed it. It all seems very petty, as if he is trying to make a point that he's in charge; he'll find his feet and things will settle down. He'll get his promotion and it'll all be fine, I've seen it all before, it'll blow over."

Andy was driving whilst Josh gathered his thoughts about how to manage the meeting that was fast approaching. This was by far the more pressing issue occupying his mind at that time. He looked at the clock in the centre of the dark grey dashboard, 10.46hrs. They would just about make it on time to the coffee shop; it would be the usual routine with Kayne. Andy and Josh would park up, go inside and buy a coffee, then Josh would phone Kayne who would park his white van in a road close by. He did this to ensure his van would not been seen in the coffee shop car park so no one would suspect he was there. This was basic tradecraft. Josh would then tell him to go inside the shop, and if he was fine with the situation and didn't recognise anyone else in the shop apart from him and Andy, he could join them at their table. Andy would then go and get Kayne his usual coffee – a latte – come back and sit down with them. It was not the most complicated of anti-surveillance routes, but they had settled in to a routine with Kayne over the last couple of years, and both parties were comfortable with it. It was perhaps not the true textbook way of meeting an informant but it worked and hadn't let them down. It made Kayne feel relaxed for the meeting and Josh didn't mind meeting him there. It was far away from where he lived and it worked, as he could fit a meeting in with Josh whilst he delivered parcels on his round. He worked for a courier company on a zero hours contract and had to take the work as and when it was offered, not an ideal situation but it helped pay the bills and wasn't exactly hard work.

Kayne had been recruited by Josh following an arrest for burglary. Kayne had broken into his ex-girlfriend's house when she was at work and stolen his clothes after she'd had the locks changed. It was not Kayne's house and he didn't take very much, but it was technically a burglary and he was convicted for it. Kayne didn't have a lot of form but was well-connected across Dorshire within the criminal world. He was clever and slippery – that why he didn't have much form. Some petty crime in his teens, but he'd learned from that about how not to get caught; keep your mouth shut and do crime by yourself. He was now 26 with a seven-year-old son from a short-lived teenage romance. He was trying to go straight but needed the money; it's not cheap trying to bankroll a single bloke's lifestyle without regular work. It was late January and the work on the building sites had slowed to such an extent that he had taken up the new role as a courier. Whatever work he did was all a bit hit and miss anyway, as Kayne was not always the most reliable employee there had ever been.

Josh had met Kayne three years ago after he had been interviewed for the burglary whilst he was in his custody cell waiting to be bailed. Josh had offered him money for grassing on those he knew in the criminal world and at that moment had really appealed to Kayne. Josh had found him just at the right time - when he was vulnerable. Grassing was a way of making easy money for passing on information he came across in his everyday life. It was a very simple business model – he would give information and Josh would write it down. Kayne would then get paid - simple. No one suspected Kayne of being a grass; he was a very likeable lad, trusted and respected. A jack-the-lad type who knew a lot of people in and around Padmouth, but now and again would do the odd thing which wasn't quite straight, to get some money and to keep credibility amongst his criminal mates. He knew that being a grass was not the safest occupation in the world, but he trusted Josh and Andy to keep him safe. They hadn't done anything that had caused him harm and he had earned a few quid out of it.

He had liked Josh the first time he had met him when he was visited in his cell. They had something in common, which was keeping fit and body-building, and they had hit it off from the beginning. Josh had been true to his word and had given him a bit of money for the intelligence and results that Kayne had provided. These were results in terms of houses that were raided on the back of information from him, and then drugs that were subsequently seized. Informants are paid on results, and the more that is seized by the police the bigger the reward for the informant.

Kayne had been earmarked as a high-risk informant as he sailed quite close to the wind and Josh was not quite sure about his true motivation. It was definitely the money he wanted, but he thought he might have been trying to provide information about things that were getting in the way of his criminal enterprises, something Josh had never quite got to the bottom of discovering. Kayne was never going to be rich out of being an informant, so Josh was very wary of his true motivation.

Josh and Andy arrived at the coffee shop and parked up. Josh always reversed into a space; you never knew what might happen during a meeting with an informant that might cause you to need to make a quick get-away. They got out of the car, walked briskly across the car park and went in. Josh looked at his watch. It was 10.58hrs and they had just made it on time. They walked a few yards into the coffee shop and looked around. It was very quiet and unusually so for a Monday. Normally the place was busy with mums with babies meeting up and having a natter over a coffee, but today seemed different. Josh and Andy went to the counter and ordered their drinks. They didn't have to queue as the morning rush was over. They were served quickly and after a few minutes took their drinks and found a table in the corner away from the window where they couldn't be overheard. They needed a good view of the door so that they could see Kayne arriving as well as anyone else coming in after him that either he or they recognised, or indeed anyone else who they deemed to be suspicious.

They sat down at a round table. Josh liked round tables as it made everyone feel equal; he was like that in life, everyone was on a level. No-one was better than anyone else and everyone was able to see and hear each other.

"Alright?" he said to Andy. "Yep. Just made it in time but it looks clear to me. Let's do it." Josh picked up his phone. He dialled Kayne's number and listened to the ring tone repeat itself. "No reply. I'll try again." He rang again, and the same thing happened. "Not like him. He's like clockwork normally, I'll give it two minutes and try again." Josh worried when this happened, as he didn't fancy getting a rollicking from Jim if any his informants failed to turn up to a meeting, which they hadn't done yet during Jim's tenure as his boss, but seeing him earlier made him a bit on edge.

Josh and Andy were just going to start talking about the weekend's football results to kill a bit of time when Josh's answer-service beeped. "That will be Kayne running late. Maybe it's the motorway traffic, it's holding everyone up today," Josh mused. He checked his text. "Yep. It's him okay." Josh phoned Kayne back.

"What's up?" he said. "Sorry," Kayne answered. "Running a bit late. Be with you in five." "See you soon," replied Josh. The line went dead. "Not like him," he said to Andy. "He sounded a bit flustered on the phone. He's given me some cracking jobs recently with some brilliant results. It makes you wonder how he's got hold of that sort of information. I've told him a million times not to get too close to it all otherwise he'll end up getting nicked." "Seen it before," said Andy knowingly. "That's how Lee Heavney ended up doing a stretch inside. I told him until I was blue in the face about getting too close but look what happened. Caught doing that ATM job in Midway last Christmas and got captured, silly boy."

They both then turned towards the door and saw Kayne walking in. He had a big grin across his face as he came towards them, yet at the same time he seemed a bit more on edge than usual. He was wearing a dark blue hoodie and blue jogging bottoms. The dirty white trainers finished off the near-criminal look; in fact this was the look he always had, slightly street fashionable but more in the style one of his many criminal mates would wear. His black hair was tidy and swept over to the right side of his head. He hadn't shaved for a couple of days sporting a bit of stubble, nothing of the designer sort though; also he had a touch of the not-having-washed-for-a-few-days smell about him.

"Latte ?" said Andy. "Yes please, sweet." "Sweet? You don't normally take sugar!" exclaimed Andy. "Idiot," said Kayne. "and can I have it in a take-away cup please?" Andy walked over to the counter to place the order. Before Josh could say anything to him Kayne leaned over the table. "Josh, listen. I've got something for you. It's bloody good but at the same time it's not good. You promise not to tell anyone, well, apart from Andy." "What is it?" asked Josh "and you know it depends on *what* you tell me; nothing you've gone and done, I hope. You know the rules and you know I must tell you this so don't get insulted. Don't tell *anyone* what you are doing, don't set anyone up and don't commit crime." "It's easy," said Josh. "Yes, yes. I know all that. It's not that, it's about bent coppers. I've been told about not just one, but a few," Kayne said furtively looked genuinely worried. "Okay, that's cool. Look, I've had this before, and it normally doesn't come to anything," said Josh. "I'll take it down and I promise that it won't go any further than it needs to."

At that point Andy came back to the table with Kayne's latte. "Thanks," said Kayne. Josh carried on. "Right. So, what have you got?" Kayne then started his story. "So I was out three nights ago round Kyle's house in Padmouth. We were having a few bevvies watching the match on the tele and shouting about the rubbish that United were playing. Kyle was there with Callum and

Haydn; they're his runners. So we'd had a few and Callum was banging on about how he thought he'd been seen picking stuff up from the boot of a car the week before at the service station by the traffic police on the M32. The police looked like they had clocked the car that he'd got into and that he might now get some attention. He reckoned he could find out whether he was going to get his house spun by some people they knew. Like people on the *inside*, like in the police. They were all very cool about it as if they'd had those type of checks done before, and they were really confident that they could find out again." "Did you get any more information like the names of people who do the checks and things like that?" said Josh. "No, you can't get anything like that. I'd just show out. Do you think I'm bloody *stupid* or something?" demanded Kayne. "Okay. Sorry, I didn't mean it to come across like that," said Josh. "If you do get anything else, like mobile numbers, or maybe even at a push the names of people that can get the checks done, that would be great. I can't do much with the information at the moment, but if you get anything else can you let me know as soon as possible, thanks." "And have you got anything else?" put in Andy. "No. Not today. Short and sweet. I'm running late and got to shoot off, sorry about that." Kayne stood up and grabbed his latte in the cardboard take-away cup. "I'm really sorry, but I've gotta go, gonna to be late otherwise. The company can check where I am in the van and they'll be on to me soon if I don't get going. I'll give you a bell in a couple of days." He went to walk away from the table where they were all sitting. "Okay, right. Don't forget the rules – don't commit crime, don't tell anyone what you are doing, and don't set anyone up! The usual!" Josh reminded him in a low voice. "Yes, yes," said Kayne and he walked off towards the door, put his hoodie over his head and went out.

"What was *that* all about?" asked Andy. "Mmm. He's talking about bent coppers, no names or anything else at the moment, and it could be a load of old rubbish. Who knows? I'll run it past Martin and see what he says. Come on, better go. Don't want to get into any more trouble with the boss today. Next, he'll be checking the cameras to see where we've got to; it's like living with Big Brother and all that. He just doesn't trust us and will even less after today, what with the breakfast fiasco. What shall we call it? I know. Breakfast-gate!"

Josh and Andy got up and looked behind them to make sure that they hadn't left anything on the table. As they walked out of the coffee shop they could see Kayne driving his van off at speed from where he had parked it. Josh thought to himself as he got in the car, he'd never dealt with information about corruption before. He had bluffed Kayne as he didn't want to be seen not to be able to manage him, and had tried to put Kayne at ease by playing it down. At the same time, he was secretly excited, yet it didn't seem quite real. He was so far from getting anywhere with it he suspected, no one would be very interested. There was no real detail yet, and it seemed quite scary to think there were some meant to be on his side in Dorshire Police who were giving away secrets to the other side. He drove a short distance before saying to Andy, "So have you dealt with corruption stuff before like he just mentioned?" "Yes," said Andy, "A few times. It's not nice stuff. Bloody grief if you ask me. You can't be too careful about who you tell and can trust, a bloody nightmare." The journey back to the office was all a bit subdued; Josh had had a reality check. He'd just been exposed to something he didn't like but knew he had to get on with it. He had been warned he might be dealing with this type of information before he joined CO15, but this was now very real. This was about possible corruption that was being carried out in his own force.

Chapter 5

Martin, Michelle, Helen and Ellie returned to the office after breakfast. There wasn't much conversation between them as they walked in. They knew the boss wasn't best pleased with them over what had just happened, but they had gotten used to him over the last couple of weeks. There were further cost-cutting measures to come to the force and they couldn't afford to upset him too much. He was largely in control of their futures and had some sway with the senior ranks in the force when it came to reducing costs. If they upset Jim too much then they would be not doing themselves any favours.

Martin went to his desk and sat down in his chair which was nearest to Jim's office. He started typing at his computer. Michelle, Helen and Ellie did the same at their desks. Nothing was said. Three quarters of an hour passed and apart from the occasional "Everyone alright?" quip from Martin, they all just got on with their work. Josh and Andy were out meeting their informant: they would be some time.

They knew when Jim was approaching the office as they could hear the floorboards creaking; the way they were creaking now. The door to the office opened and in he walked. He had a face like thunder. Either the meeting he had just come from had been a bad one, or he was still in a rage about the team disobeying him by going for breakfast. He walked briskly towards his office, took his off jacket and sat down in his chair. He started flicking through some paperwork he'd left on his desk. The only noise you could hear from the rest of the team in the main office was that of their fingers typing away on keyboards. The tension was palpable.

Helen hated this type of situation. It made her nervous and she could not concentrate on her work. Michelle, meanwhile did not care. She had met Jim's type before and nothing fazed her. Martin was equally relaxed. He was getting paid regardless of who his boss was or how they acted. It was hardly the most heinous of crimes he had sanctioned that had been committed – having a team breakfast. The team knew that Jim had obviously got the hump. It was like working with a spoilt child who had to have his own way regardless of how ridiculous he made himself look - and all because he was a DI and he was in charge.

Helen stood up. "Michelle, do you fancy going for a bit of fresh air? I just need a few things for dinner," she said. "Sounds like a great idea. I need to get a few extra things too. You coming, Martin?" Michelle said. "No, thanks," he replied. "Too much to do. Enjoy!" "You coming, Ellie?" Helen asked. "Oh yes. I could do with a break from the screen." Any excuse to get away from the terrible atmosphere in the office and Ellie jumped at the chance. Helen put on her coat and Ellie and Michelle did the same. "Are you sure you don't want anything, Martin?" Helen queried. "No thanks. I'm on a strict diet," he explained. "Anything for you, boss?" Helen addressed Jim. "Not for me," he answered, without looking up and carrying on typing. Michelle and Helen left the office. They glanced at Martin and raised their eyebrows. Martin winked at them as they departed.

Just then Martin's phone rang. It was Josh. "Alright," he said. "You okay?" "Yep. All good," Josh said. "Kayne turned up but we didn't have long with him today. He didn't have too much to give, but what he did might be of interest. Will let you know when we get back. I'd rather not talk about it over the phone." "Alright, catch up soon." He placed his mobile phone back on his desk and resumed typing. He could hear Jim typing too. Nothing more was said and the silence continued.

Another twenty minutes passed. The two carried on typing, the tense silence broken by the sound of a door closing somewhere else on the same corridor they shared with other teams in the department. Jim got up from his desk. He was a man of few words but even fewer today. He stretched his arms above his head; he was irked and he was rattled. Something had got to him. He could see Martin a few yards away sitting at his desk tapping away on his keyboard. Martin was a strong character and had the ear of the team. Jim knew this, and that he wasn't liked by the CO15 team. He could tell they didn't like him by their reaction to him every time they saw him, but it didn't bother him. His arrogance ensured that. He also didn't care what they thought. He had reached the rank of DI and the team knew that what he said, went. The police is a very rank-structured organisation and Jim was very much of the old-school way of doing things. He knew he held the power in the office and consequently over the team. He also felt that if he could break Martin he would have even more control over them. He had worked with this type of junior supervisor before and his method of asserting control in the past, getting rid of people, had worked for him. He would employ his tried and tested technique he'd used before to great effect.

Jim knew there was no one else in the office. There was just the two of them, alone. Jim picked up his jacket from the back of his chair and slipped it on. He picked up his black leather briefcase and walked out of his office which was in the corner of the room. He walked quietly up behind Martin and whispered to him over his shoulder. "You shouldn't crack onto a senior officer's wife. You'll pay for this." Martin looked around and saw Jim walking off towards the door with his back to him. Jim didn't turn round. He leaned down to the left of the door and his swipe card beeped as it allowed him to exit the office before he disappeared down the corridor. The office door closed slowly and Martin heard it thud shut.

Martin sat there alone in the office. He sat at his desk in disbelief. He looked straight ahead. Had he just heard what he thought he had heard? What was it Jim had just said? "You shouldn't crack onto a senior officer's wife. You'll pay for this." Martin repeated this over and over again in his head and then out loud. What did he mean? What was he going on about? Could his boss really have said this to him? And why would he have done it? *What* could he have possibly meant? Then it started to dawn on him. Lorraine was Jim's wife. She was a lovely person, chatty and bubbly and Martin had recently met her again, albeit very briefly and had got on with her. Not that he knew her apart from a course they had been on years ago and more recently in the pub and in the canteen earlier. But there was nothing in it. Martin didn't know her at all. He was happily married and would in no way "crack onto" Jim's wife.

What?! He was in disbelief. Then he had a thought. Maybe this was Jim's way of trying to break him, to unsettle him so he would leave the team and Jim could bring in someone he knew and wanted in the role. Jim could then mould the supervisor, and tell him what to do without any questions. He pondered a bit more but was still in disbelief. Who could he tell, and who would believe him? Who would ever believe that an Inspector would say and do such a thing? Just keep it to yourself he thought, think it over and then decide what to do. Never make a decision in haste. Sleep on it, he thought, and then take some action. He was in shock.

Just then Martin could hear Josh and Andy approaching the office again; the floorboards had started to creak. The office door opened. "Alright lads?" Martin asked. "How'd it go?" Martin was good at bluffing. He had learned, and then honed it as a skill over the years. It didn't come naturally to him, but he'd gradually perfected it as just one of many attributes of the role of an informant handler. He couldn't let on to the team what had just happened with Jim. It would have made them despise him even more. "Yep. All good," said Andy. Josh winked at Martin. Martin knew what was coming. "Well, sort of," amended Josh. "We need a word. Have you got five minutes?" "Of course," said Martin. "Fire away."

Josh looked round the office to make sure nobody else was in and asked, "Are we alone? There's definitely no one else here?" "Yep," averred Martin. "What have you got?" Josh was nervous. "It's like this. Kayne was rattling on today about people on the inside, inside the police, like doing corruption. It's all a bit unnerving. I've never come across stuff like this before. What to do, eh?" Martin sat back in his chair. He had dealt with informants talking about corruption before and knew just what to do with this type of information. He knew that he had to keep it as tight as possible and make sure no one else found out. There was no way anyone could find out about it. Corruption spreads to every corner of every organisation and Dorshire Police was no exception. He had dealt with corruption in other agencies as well, and was ably versed in how to deal with it. That was one of the reasons he was in the role. CO15 dealt with informants who had historically provided information about corruption and Martin had close ties with Dorshire's Anti-Corruption Unit. He had long held them in high regard as he had the highest of ethical standards and they were there to uphold them. There was nothing in life Martin despised more than those he worked with giving secrets away to those he was to catch and then convict. What was the point of him turning up to work just for someone to betray his and his team's trust? Not only that, but it increased the danger to him, his team and the informants they worked so hard to protect. It was a dangerous business at the best of times, but to have corrupt officers giving away secrets just heightened the danger.

Martin got Josh to repeat what had happened at the meeting and scribbled down a few notes. "Listen. You know how much I hate this type of thing. It just goes against the grain; it's bang out of order. The best thing to do is this. Don't write anything down just yet; no Contact Sheets or discussion with anyone else – not even Michelle or Helen at the moment." "And the boss?" Josh enquired. "Um...not even him, either," said Martin. "When I mean keep it tight, I mean keep it *really* tight. I'll get across to the Anti-Corruption Unit in a minute and let you know what they say. This sort of thing ain't easy to deal with but it is what it is. We'll get it sorted, don't worry." Josh seemed a bit more at ease. He trusted Martin with what he was saying and doing. He would just sit tight and see what unfolded.

Martin wasn't one to sit around. He got up from his desk and walked towards the door; he'd briefly forgotten what Jim had said to him. His opinion of Jim wasn't great anyway after what had happened earlier that morning, and Jim was rapidly dwindling in his estimation. Besides, this issue was far more important. Martin wasn't a career Detective Sergeant, he just loved his job to the point he wanted to do it to the best of his ability. He was very proud of his small team and what they'd achieved. He knew the value of reputation and wasn't going to let Jim derail his day. As he walked towards the door he turned to Josh and Andy. They were both sitting at their desks and had started looking through their bags to see what they had each brought into work for lunch. They both looked up as Martin spoke. "You know how I hate this sort of stuff. It really gets to my soul." They could see just how much Martin was fired up. He was a man of his word and a man of integrity. "I'm just off to see the Anti-Corruption Unit. I don't know how long I'll be, but if the boss asks just say I've popped to the shops for some lunch. If he gets back just text me to give me some warning. Thanks." Martin turned and walked out of the office. Josh and Andy looked at each other and started eating their lunch. They knew Martin of old. He was not afraid of anything and knew he had the bit between his teeth again.

Chapter 6

DCI Keith Catlin picked up his phone. It was Monday lunchtime and he was getting hungry. He had been at work for a few hours and already it was turning into one of those weeks. He'd had two meetings that morning and taken so many phone calls he could already do with another weekend off. He was the DCI in the Anti-Corruption Unit and had been in the post for four years. There wasn't much he hadn't seen, and nothing really surprised him in terms of the wrongdoing officers and staff had done in Dorshire Police. He was 54 and hadn't got very long at all to go before he retired. He was counting down the weeks until he could put his feet up. He could already smell the freshly cut grass on his local golf course he longed to play on every day, and was desperate to lower his handicap. His wife had put up with a lot during his career and it was time they spent more time together. His children had grown up and left home. It was going to be his time again.

The phone on his desk rang yet again. He answered it in his gruff Welsh accent. "Hello. DCI Catlin." "Boss. It's Rob, downstairs. You got five minutes, please? I need to show you something." "Is it important?" Keith asked. "I've got a lot on this morning already." "Yes, guv. It looks important to me." "Okay, pop up." Rob Boakes was a Detective Constable who had worked in the Anti-Corruption Unit for 8 years. He was an experienced officer who knew risk when he came across it. His work was impeccable and he was trusted to do the right thing. Rob was a very square peg in a very round hole. A minute later Rob knocked on Keith's door. "Come in." He walked into Keith's office, closed the door and sat in a comfortable beige chair in front of the desk. Rob looked over his shoulder towards the door. He wanted to make sure it had stayed closed. "Are you expecting anyone, boss?" Rob queried. "No," answered Keith. "What's up?" "Just got this in," said Rob, waving a Dorshire Police A4-sized intelligence report in the air. He leaned across the desk towards Keith and slid the report swiftly towards him. Keith put on his reading glasses, picked up the report and started to read it. "Dave is a PC based in Padmouth working on the multi-agency neighbourhood unit. He is telling his friends outside of the police about search warrants that are near to happening. Around three weeks ago, he told a friend about a search that was going to take place, and a gun disappeared before the police turned up; they found nothing. In the past he has given information to his brother who sells drugs in the town, his brother having been to prison for selling drugs, but is still selling them." Having read the report and read it again Keith looked up. "Dave Harrison? So? What's new? We've had this sort of stuff on Harrison before and haven't got anywhere with it. We've wasted so much time on him, it's probably the usual load of old gossip. Just do the usual checks and we'll go from there." "Yes, boss, okay, but the twist is this. The information came in over the weekend on the confidential hotline; the informant says her name is Susan. She claims she's a female relative of Dave, so it's probably the closest we've ever had anyone to him." "And? So what's new? We haven't got the resources to do anything with any decent information anyway," replied Keith. Even though he knew no one had come into the office since he'd arrived, Rob nervously looked around again just in case there was anyone there. "But Dave is a good friend of DI Jim Fowler from CO15. If we give this to him to see what he thinks about one of the his team contacting Susan, he'll know that someone is talking about Dave. I'm not saying that Jim is bent, or even Dave, but just to keep it nice and tidy..." Rob trailed off. He was thinking he had said a bit too much about the tactics Keith should employ as well as making aspersions about two police officers in the force, one of whom was a middle manager. "Just saying," he concluded.

Keith looked at Rob. He knew Rob well having worked with him a lot over the years and thought highly of his most experienced intelligence officer. He sat in his chair and played with a biro that he had been chewing, tapping the gnarled end gently on the wooden table. Nothing was said whilst he pondered his problem. "Mmm. Difficult one. I know what you're saying, but you can see where this is going. If I don't let Jim have a look at assessing this, then I'm virtually saying he can't be trusted. If I do, then I'm potentially giving him a way of tipping off Dave and preventing us from catching him. God. Never had this before. Difficult one.

"I'll have a think. Keep it tight and I'll let you know. Who else knows in the team?" "No one, guv. I've only just checked the hotline and found the voicemail on an e-mail in there," said Rob. "Let's keep it that way and don't tell anyone. I'll think it over," said Keith. "Have you got anything else we know about Susan?" "She phoned the hotline and left her number but didn't give her full name. She's happy for someone to speak to her, but no one has as yet," replied Rob standing up. As he turned to walk out of the office, he asked,

"Anything from the shop, guv?" Keith was starving.

"Thought you wouldn't ask! A meal deal, please. Cheese and onion sarnie, crisps and any drink — ta. I'll give you the money when you get back. Cheers."

Rob nodded, walked out of the office and closed the door behind him.

Keith stood up and wandered towards the window that was to the right of the comfy chair. He looked out and saw Martin, the DS from CO15 in the main car park of the headquarters complex. He could see he was chatting to two female colleagues, one of whom he recognised as Michelle but didn't know the other. Martin and Keith had worked together a long time ago, but Martin hadn't been interested in promotion and so carried on managing informants. He had a lot of respect for Martin who he regarded as knowing his stuff. If there was anyone in Dorshire Police that he trusted, it was Martin. Martin had worked on several investigations involving corrupt officers and there wasn't much he hadn't seen from an informant perspective. Keith wandered back to his seat and sat down again. He was bothered. This was a problem he didn't need, particularly today. He had so many other things to do, but this issue had the potential to become massive if he didn't make the right call in how to deal with it.

Just as he had started typing the report he needed for a meeting that afternoon, there was a knock on his door. "Come on in," he called. It was Martin. "Morning, Sir. You got five minutes? Won't take long." Martin smiled when he called him 'Sir'. It was only at work he called him 'Sir' and this was certainly not the case down the pub when they were off-duty. Keith sighed. "This better be important. I've had a gutful already today!" "Yeah. Same here," said Martin. "You ready for this?" Keith sighed again. "Go on. Surprise me."

Martin sat down in the comfy beige chair in front of Keith's desk and started telling him about the report Josh had given him earlier; the issue relating to possible corruption in the force and the leaking of information to Kyle, Callum and Haydn. Martin was very good and never revealed who the informant handler was, let alone the informant. "And how good is this informant? Not one of your dodgy ones?" enquired Keith. "Bang on. Been on the books for a couple of years. They're always right," said Martin.

Keith looked at Martin. "You know something? You always give me a headache but this time you might just have knocked on my door at the right time. Do you know anything about those three?" Martin shook his head. "Nope. They are just names to me." Keith looked at Martin again. "Padmouth seems to have started to be a bit more of a problem recently and could do with some work being done on it. What's the capacity in your team like?" Martin thought for a moment. "It's not too bad although we're struggling a bit to get Jim to agree to payments, and the sources are slowly dropping off the books cos he keeps cancelling them. Why?" Keith began speaking more quietly. "It's just that I've got the name of someone who might be able to help with a job which has been rumbling on for a few years; we never seem to have gotten anywhere with it. They want to talk about a PC called Dave who works in Padmouth, but it's all a bit sensitive really. This might be tied into what you are talking about. Have you got 10 minutes?" "Of course mate. Anything for you." Keith continued. "The problem I've got is, that

Dave is a good friend of Jim's and if this name went in front of him to assess, I don't know whether he would get the team to rate them as an informant. Jim could, and I'm not saying he would, let Dave know someone wants to talk about him. You see what I'm saying?" Martin nodded. "Yep, got it," he said. "So what do you think? Not to tell Jim and just get someone else outside of the force to manage them?" Keith sat back in his chair. "I'm thinking that *you* do it. You and the team *without* Jim knowing." "What?" gasped Martin. "Run someone behind Jim's back without him knowing. Do you think I'm mad? He doesn't really like the team anyway; if he found out, he would go absolutely spare.". Keith looked at Martin. "Listen, I get it; it's not really a runner is it? So have you got any better ideas?" Martin thought for a while. "What about this? If you just give the report without the details of the informant, just the information to Jim and see what he says, then it may help in deciding what we should do. That way it doesn't give too much away and protects Susan, but we'll be able to gauge by what Jim does and how he reacts." "Like it!" exclaimed Keith. "Yes. I like it a lot. I'll give him a bell and meet up with him. If you could see if your source can get any more about Kyle and his mates, that would be great, thanks. Keep us updated and I'll let you know what happens once I've told Jim."

Martin thought about Keith's part of the plan. Although he and Keith went back a long way and he was going behind Jim's back, Keith was the boss now for this job and the whole thing would be his project; it was Keith's idea and he was responsible for it. That suited Martin just fine; Keith was a higher rank than Jim, and Martin had top cover. "Cool," said Martin. "I'll give you a bell."

"Oh, and just to confirm, I won't tell Jim about the stuff we got on Kyle and his mates either. Just in case it's all part of the same thing. You never know with this sort of investigation." "Mum's the word," agreed Keith. Martin got up from the comfy chair. "Sorted. Love this. Let's get rid of the bent sods." He closed the door behind him as he left Keith's office.

Keith looked at the intelligence report again and studied every word for a third, fourth and fifth time. He kept reading the words as if they actually meant something tangible. There had been so many occasions when he had read intelligence reports that were just malicious, trying to stitch up coppers, but this one seemed to be more realistic; it seemed to mean more. He could get research done on the recent search warrants carried out in Padmouth, and could gather some background information on Harrison. Not only that, but he could have some research done on Kyle, Callum and Haydn to see if they had any links to him too. It just all seemed that the timing of these two reports was somewhat too much of a coincidence.

Keith picked up the phone. "Rob, it's Keith. Can you do me a favour, please? Can you do some checks to see if Dave Harrison is linked to anyone called either Callum, Haydn or Kyle?" "What – now, boss?" Rob asked. "Yep," said Keith. Keith could hear Rob tapping away on his keyboard; he was already researching the names that Keith had given him. It didn't take long for Rob to say something. "Yep. Harrison is the officer who's investigating a shoplifting that Kyle got nicked for a month ago. Do you want me to tell you more?" "Yep. Can you let me know what happened please?" Keith requested. Rob continued reading from his screen.

"He was caught on CCTV leaving the shop but it looks as if the job isn't going anywhere." There was a bit of a silence and Rob went on, "Yep. It's been no-crimed. It's just waiting to be assessed by a supervisor and then it can be filed." "By whom?" Keith asked. "Harrison," replied Rob. "Cheers. Can you print the crime report off for me, please, and bring it up to the office? Thanks."

Keith put the phone down. There was a long way to go before he could find the reasons behind it all, and there were many questions needing answers. Keith was not a man to be beaten, and with only a few weeks left in the force he was determined that this job was one he wouldn't let get away. There was a big push to improve standards across the force and Keith was ideally placed, he was exactly the right man to make this happen regardless of the ranks that were potentially involved. Keith liked a challenge and this would be one of the biggest he had come across at the end of his thirty-year career. What a way to end it all, he mused.

Chapter 7

The team sat in the office in near silence. The only sound heard was that of them tapping away on their keyboards; they all had reports to type and plenty of them. Although Jim had cut a few of their informants from the books, they were making those that remained work even harder. The handlers knew how to get the most out of them, by getting them to report on areas of criminality that they had either previously reported on, or requiring them to spend more time and therefore provide more detail on those they had always provided information about. For some of their informants it wasn't about the money, it was about the relationship they had built up with the handlers over the years. The trust they had built with the established and most experienced members of the team had taken years to grow and nurture – it didn't just happen overnight. Michelle and Andy understood this and were frustrated by the apparent very short-term vision of Jim. Josh was newer to this type of work and although he sometimes became exasperated, he was still in the game of recruiting newer sources, like Kayne Woolery.

Michelle and Helen had returned to the office from their lunch and had spoken to Martin on their way back from the shops. "Where was Martin going?" Michelle asked Josh. "To see the Anti-Corruption Unit." "Oh," said Michelle. "Any particular reason?" Andy butted in, "Why's that?" "Well, he told us he was going to the shops to get some lunch!" Andy looked at Josh knowingly. Michelle smiled. "Go on then. What's happened"? Before Josh could answer, Andy spoke for him. "I think it's probably best for Martin to speak for himself; he'll be back in a moment." Josh felt a bit embarrassed. He was the newest member of the team and had forgotten Martin had told him to keep it tight, including keeping it tight even within the team. "I'm sorry to have put us all in a position; my fault," he said. There was a bit of an eerie silence. "Look, let's wait until Martin gets back," said Michelle. "He'll explain what's happened. No one has done anything particularly wrong, it's just a misunderstanding, I'm sure."

The team carried on writing their reports. Helen was in the furthest corner of the office and wasn't listening as she had her earphones in whilst she processed the team's reports. The office door opened. It was Martin.

He looked slightly perturbed. "Right, team. A quick meeting please." He walked over to Ellie and asked her to join in. "Right. Just a quick meeting before Jim gets back from wherever he has gone. And if he comes back, we will change the subject and talk about the...um...the holiday leave requests for next year. Right. Josh and Andy had a meeting with Woolery this morning. He was talking about a possible corruption...." Josh cut him short. "Sarge. I've something to say. Michelle knows that you went to see the Anti-Corruption Unit instead of going to the shops and..." Martin looked at Josh. "Right. What did I say about..." Josh just nodded with a degree of embarrasment. "Anyway, it's like this. DCI Keith Catlin is really interested in what Woolery is saying, as it ties in with another job that they've got going on. Josh, can you put a call in to

Kayne after this meeting, please, and get another meeting on with him tomorrow morning? I want full cover on the meeting and a full debrief with him. When you speak to him in a minute, I need him to get round to see Callum and his mates tonight and get more out of them. I need telephone numbers, registrations and names — the whole shooting match. Everything he can possibly get. If the boss asks how you got on this morning, just say he cancelled on you last minute and you have re-arranged the meeting for tomorrow. Whatever you do, don't say a bloody thing to make him suspicious. Any questions?" "Any chance of a few quid to keep him happy?" Andy asked. "30 quid for his petrol," said Martin. "Is that it?" Andy said. "Yep. Jim will start asking too many questions, otherwise," replied Martin. He is tighter than a gnat's chuff. Listen. Woolery is coming up with some good stuff. I don't need any grief from the guvnor. He's watching us like a hawk and I don't need any excuse for him to cut Woolery."

Martin looked at his watch; it was 1.38pm. The team went home at 4pm and there was still a lot to do that day. He didn't know where Jim had got to but he hadn't forgotten what he had said to him earlier. His words were troubling Martin. He was wondering what he could have possibly meant. Martin had never made a single pass at a senior officer's wife. To whom could he have been referring? Maybe Lorraine? But he had only seen her twice in ten years and that was in the last four days; once on Friday and again this morning on the ill-fated mission to have breakfast. Jim was playing mind games. If he was trying to get him to leave the team by pressurising him so he could not stand working with him, he was truly mistaken. Martin was not a man to be turned and bullied out of his role. Jim was new to this team and although he was the boss, he would not let him ruin what was a great team. He suspected Jim wanted his ally Paul Slacke to take his role but Martin was not going anywhere. He had a small but very professional team and no one was going to break their team spirit. It took a lot to run a team of informant handlers and there was a good deal of stress involved. Jim didn't understand this having never been in covert policing, let alone informant handling. But on the other hand Martin was a forgiving sort. He understood Jim was new to the role. He thought long and hard about Jim and the sort of pressure he was feeling. Thinking about it a bit more he didn't want the bad feeling in the office to continue, and decided that it would take time to get to know Jim. They would try to get him to see how they could make things work and achieve the results for his promotion. They would eventually win him round with their results; they would show him what they could do. They just had to get over the small issue of breakfast that morning and keep this corruption issue under wraps for a few days, then things would settle down. Maybe there was nothing in it, and it was another piece of spurious reporting as Keith said he frequently came across in the Anti-Corruption Unit. Martin was ever the optimist. It would all work out for the best in the long run, he thought.

Chapter 8

Keith pondered what to do next. He knew he had to do something to try to uncover the truth of what was going on, but had to tread very carefully. He knew Jim from the old days when they had worked in Major Crime together. He knew he was a dour figure with few friends, but also knew that he was no fool. He was experienced within the investigative world but was aware that he had no covert policing experience. It was therefore imperative he made his next move swiftly and without arousing suspicion. Although he felt slightly uncomfortable doing what he had agreed to do with Martin, he was still going behind the back of Jim who was a colleague and a middle manager, and to whom he was going to be less than 100% truthful with all the facts. Nonetheless he had to do what he had to do, and he had to do it decisively. He decided to call Jim there and then and meet him to discuss the sensitive information that had come into Rob's inbox that morning.

"Afternoon, Jim. It's Keith Catlin. You okay?" They made small talk and Keith invited Jim across to his office to view the intelligence report. He had had it sanitised and carefully read it and re-read it to ensure that the name of the informant had been removed and was nowhere to be seen. "Yes. What, right now?" Jim said. "Of course. I'm just in Paul Slacke's office. I'll be with you in 10." Keith chewed over in his head what he thought Jim's reaction might be and went through all the different permutations. At best Jim would take stock of the information and ask if there were any details about the source and who was the informant. At worst, Jim may dismiss the report as nonsense and put Keith in a very awkward position to try and progress the intelligence. There was no real middle ground apart from Jim declaring his knowledge of Dave Harrison and letting a team from another force manage the informant. What to do, Keith thought.

Keith looked out of his window and saw Jim walking purposefully across the headquarters car park from the direction of the Traffic Process Unit. It wasn't long before there was a knock on his door. "Come in," Keith called. It was Jim. "Come in. Take a seat," and pointed towards the comfy chair in front of his desk. "Thanks," replied Jim, and sat down. "Thanks for coming over so quickly, Jim," Keith began. "Something came in this morning that might be of interest to you. It's information about a PC Dave Harrison whose is based in Padmouth. I don't know if you remember him from your days there?" "Dave — of course. What is it? What's this about, then?" asked Jim. "Have a look at this" said Keith, and slid the copy of the intelligence report across his desk to Jim. Jim picked it up and read it slowly. He smiled. "Dave? Never. What would he do those things for? I'd trust him with my life. Where did you get this crap from?" he asked. "Anonymous. Get this sort of stuff all the time," explained Keith. "Nothing in it," Jim insisted. "It's all crap, he'd never do anything like that." "Good enough for me" Keith assured him. "I knew it was worth giving you a bell. That's it. Nothing else. Short and sweet!" "That's *it*?" Jim repeated. "Got off my butt and came across here for that rubbish? Next time you get anything half decent, let me know," and laughed with Keith. "I couldn't do your job" Jim continued. "Trudging through that load of rubbish every day. You ain't got too long left, have you? Count down the days and this will all seem like a bad memory soon! Look, I've got to get back to where I was with Paul and help him finish a report he is doing. Anything else you need, just give me a bell." With that he got up and shook Keith's hand. He walked across the office towards the door and closed it behind him.

Keith just sat in his seat dumbfounded. Jim had not reacted the way he thought he would by being honest with him. Keith knew that Jim had hardly any experience in the covert world and Jim always knew best. Maybe he genuinely thought that it was a load of old rubbish, or maybe Jim would now tell Harrison the details he had just read on the intelligence report – that there was someone talking about him. Keith's problem had just grown bigger. Did he believe Jim in saying there was no substance to the report and that he was calling his bluff?

Jim left Keith's office and hurried down the stairs. He had a bit of a walk across the car park to get back to Paul's office. The car park was crammed and there was very little space to walk between the parked cars. Jim took his mobile phone out of his left trouser pocket. He looked around and scrolled through his contacts. He found the number on his phone he was looking for and pressed the green call button. The phone went straight to answer-message. "Alright. It's me. Give me a bell when you are free. Cheers." Jim put the phone back into his left trouser pocket and carried on towards Paul's office.

Chapter 9

The next day was Tuesday. It was another rainy day. It seemed it had been raining for most of January and didn't help lift the mood in the office. It was early morning and Martin's team drifted into work. They were meant to start the day at 8am but were all in and at their desks by 7.55am. Jim usually came in about 8.20am so they normally had to be at work to catch up and make small talk before he came in. He had only been their boss for a couple of weeks, but they seemed to have the measure of him. He was a man of few words, and so far had seemed to let Martin get on and run the office. As they came into work they all chatted about the night before and asked each other how they were. They were a friendly bunch and enjoyed each other's company.

It was 8am, and Martin knew that he had a bit of time before Jim arrived to consider what he wanted to say, and more importantly what he couldn't say in the morning briefing. "Listen guys, I've been thinking. It's probably best if we don't tell Jim about the possible corruption information that Kayne told Josh yesterday. You know these things have a habit of getting blown up out of all proportion by managers, so I think it's best if we keep it really tight. Like I mean so tight that he doesn't know – just for the moment until we get it all bottomed out and boxed off. So when we have the briefing, Josh, you say that Kayne didn't turn up yesterday and that he needs to meet you again today, that he has something urgent to give you but doesn't want to give it over the phone." Josh wasn't used to the sort of strategy Martin was advocating and started to speak, but Martin cut him off. "I know, I know. Listen. I don't like doing this but it's for the best. You have to trust me with this one. If it all goes wrong, then on my head be it."

Josh piped up. "Martin, if this goes wrong then I'm going to get it. In fact we are *all* going to get it from Jim, and with both barrels. He'll have it in for every one of us big time and that's no joke. I've not been here as long as the rest of the team and I don't want to lose this role, thank you very much." Michelle chipped in. "Josh, just do as he says. He is very rarely wrong and is meant to be supervising us. Anyway, take it as a lawful order and that way you know you're covered." Andy and Helen just listened and said nothing. They all were waiting for Jim to come into work.

It was 8.15am and Martin decided to start the morning meeting. "Right all. Let's get cracking with the day. Just a few admin points to go through before we find out what each other has got on today, so let's start with…" Just as he said that the office door opened, and Jim walked in. "Morning, everyone," he said as he strode towards his office in the corner of the room. "Morning, boss," said Martin, "you okay?" "Yes thanks. Carry on with the briefing. I'll listen in whilst I log on and get ready for my first meeting at 9am." Martin continued. "So, I expect all the cars to be washed and cleaned out by the end of the week, please. I know it's that time of year when they are hard to keep clean especially with the number of miles we do, but I don't want to get caught out by a snap inspection of the covert fleet. Just make sure you record your mileage too as there's a push on getting the cars in for a service at the workshops at the right time. So that's it for the mundane everyday agenda items. Let's go around the team and find out what we are all doing today. So, let's start with Josh. How did it go yesterday with Kayne? Josh coughed and said "Yep. When we arrived he wasn't there, so I put a call in to him to see where he was, and he said he was really sorry, but he couldn't make it. We agreed to meet him at the same time and place today and..." Jim chipped in from his office. "Josh. Who's running who here? You are meant to be a CO15 handler. You need to get a grip of him or this will be the last meeting you have with him, 'cos I'll get rid of him straightaway. Too much jeopardy and too much risk for not a lot of information, if any." "Okay boss," said Josh as he raised his voice to be clear to Jim that he had heard his instruction. Martin said "Right Josh. I want full cover on this meeting as he could be trying to set us up for a mighty fall. Top notch tradecraft, please. I want everyone out with all points covered to make sure not only he, but everyone else on that meeting is kept 100% safe. That's Michelle and Helen too, please. Take your Personal Protection Equipment as well." Jim chipped in again. "Everyone going out for the meeting Martin? It seems a bit of overkill." "You can never be too safe with a high-risk source, boss," he pointed out. "Sure, I'm listening. But if he's not coming up with anything, he's gone today. Make sure he fully understands that too. No ambiguity," he said sharply. "Okay," agreed Martin.

The team looked at each other as they knew Jim couldn't see them behind the wall that partitioned his office from the rest of the room. Martin continued. "So that's going to take most of the morning. When we all get back we'll have a debrief and see what happened.

You alright with it Josh?" Josh nodded. "Yep. All good to go. I'll brief everyone in a minute about where I want them to be, the route in and out of the debrief venue and all that type of stuff." Martin continued with the meeting and rounded up the other work that the team had going on. "Thanks, everyone. Have a great day." Everyone got back to their work and started typing up their contact sheets.

About half an hour had gone by and Jim's phone rang. It was Paul. "Morning" he said. "Free now? Right, I'll see you in the canteen in five minutes." With that he tidied his desk and got up. "Martin. I'm just popping downstairs before going to the 9.30 meeting. Just give me a call if you need anything." "Okay, boss," he said. The atmosphere was somewhat better today than it had been the day before. Jim seemed a bit more relaxed and there wasn't the aggressive inflection the team had picked up on the day before. This was despite the pressure the team was now under with the strict instructions Martin had given about not telling Jim what Kayne had said the day before. All was going to plan, and no-one had cracked. All the signs were good.

Now that Jim had gone to his meeting early, Martin decided to say something in addition to what he had said earlier. "Listen guys. I'm just going to say a bit more. I know this is really difficult for you all and goes against the grain, but like I said yesterday, you just have to trust me with this one. I am the most loyal copper you will ever find, but when it comes to corruption, in my experience you just can't be too safe. If anyone feels that they need a chat anytime just ask or call me. It's really no problem." The team all nodded. Not much more was said until Josh rallied them to go out in readiness to meet Kayne.

"Okay. Everyone ready to go and know what they're doing?" Josh asked. They all nodded. Michelle and Helen had been instructed to forward plot and watch Kayne drive into the car park which was closest to the coffee shop where he had met Josh and Andy the previous day. It was a car park in a supermarket and gave plenty of cover as it meant they didn't stand out.

It was agreed amongst themselves that once Kayne was in position and parked up, one of them would phone Josh and let him know that Kayne was safe and by himself. Josh would then phone Kayne and tell him to walk the short distance across the car park and go into the coffee shop. Helen would follow on foot and sit in Josh's car, which would be kept unlocked so she could keep an eye on the door of the coffee shop ensuring no one followed Kayne in. Kayne was aware that if he was to be questioned by anyone he knew as to why he was in the coffee shop, he was seeing a couple of guys who ran a local pub football team and wanted to see if he was interested in playing in their team for the rest of the season. This fitted with Kayne's lifestyle as he had played a bit of football in the past, but his enthusiasm had waned in the last few months and he was in danger of being kicked out of his local team. Everyone knew what to do and had done this route and deployed this tradecraft several times before. It was a tried and tested route and it worked.

Josh and Andy left headquarters in the covert VW Golf and Michelle and Helen left in the unmarked Vauxhall Astra. The cars were on fake company registration plates and just looked like normal cars. The team had their pepper spray and batons with them just in case it all went very wrong, but in all the years of experience the team had between them, they'd never had to use any of their protective equipment.

It wasn't too long before they had driven to the debrief area; Michelle and Helen drove into position and waited. They phoned Andy to tell him they were there, whilst at the same time Josh and Andy had taken up the same position in the coffee shop they had been in the day before. It was a textbook deployment and a well-practiced routine. It was 10.46am and they were all there in plenty of time. They waited; 11.00am came and went with no sign of Kayne. Josh was getting anxious again, just as he had been the previous day . If Kayne didn't appear Jim would surely cancel his informant status. Josh didn't want to lose Kayne, albeit he was giving him a few more headaches than he was used to; 11.12am came and went. Josh was sweating. Not again. Bloody informants, he thought.

Just then his phone rang. It was Michelle. "He's here. Yep. It's Kayne alright. He has just parked up. I'll phone you when he gets out. Helen will do the follow." Josh called Kayne again. "Alright. You in position?" "Yep," was the reply. "Do the usual and we'll see you in five. If you recognise anyone or think that you are being followed just come in, get a coffee and go back to your van. Drink your coffee and then phone me again. But you should be fine." "Okay" Kayne replied.

Michelle phoned Josh. "All good from this end, Josh. He's by himself in the van and Helen will do the follow. Phone me when you have finished the meeting." "Yep, thanks," said Josh, and hung up. Kayne didn't normally hang around once Josh had given him the go-ahead to start walking the route to the meeting venue. Helen would have a job keeping up with him. Kayne was a bit of an athlete when he was at school and didn't hang around.

The wind was increasing and there were a few odd leaves left over from the autumn that were now being blown around on the floor. Kayne got out of his van and set off at a pace. Helen walked quickly but just far enough behind Kayne to make sure he was alone and not on the phone. She had followed him on this route twice before in the last month and he had never looked round or seen her. She was good at what she did and had never been challenged. She had a job keeping up with him because recently she'd a bit of a problem with her right foot and was walking with a slight limp. Today was not the best time for her to be deployed on foot to follow Kayne, but she gritted her teeth and got on with the job in hand. Kayne looked around a couple of times as he walked along a path across a grassed area from the car park towards the coffee shop. Helen carried a large shopping bag which matched the surroundings and Kayne spotted her as he looked round but didn't suspect her of following him; he just carried on walking swiftly along the path. Helen thought that next time they followed Kayne, it would be Michelle doing the surveillance.

Helen saw Kayne approaching the coffee shop. He glanced over his left shoulder one last time as he walked in to make sure there was no one around that he knew, dressed in the same clothes he'd been wearing the day before. Despite Kayne having gone into the coffee shop Helen kept walking towards it. Josh had left the driver's door of the Golf unlocked and Helen got into the driver's seat. She had a good view of the front of the coffee shop so would be able to alert Josh and Andy if anyone suspicious approached the place. She settled into the seat and sent a text to Andy and Michelle confirming nothing untoward had happened whilst she had followed Kayne, and was now in position to cover the front of the shop. Helen settled down and turned the radio on.

Kayne walked through the door of the coffee shop and went towards Josh and Andy where they had been sitting at the same table the day before. Josh saw Kayne approach them and had made sure that he had his usual drink ready for him. "Morning. Got you your latte and there's some sugar in it" said Andy.

"Cheers," Kayne answered. He didn't seem to be in his usual jovial mood. He put his phone on the table.

"How long you got?" Josh enquired.

"All day if you want. I'm doing nothing all day. Just at home."

"Won't be that long, I hope. How much you got to tell me?" Josh asked.

"Well. Loads really," said Kayne. "Shall I start?"

Josh nodded and said, "Okay. So you went around there last night and what happened?"

"Right, it's like this. I went around to Kyle's house like you asked me to. It was about ten past eight 'cos I'd just left Callum's house having had a couple of beers. I drove round to Kyle's house to…"

"And"? said Josh. "To pick up some gear for Callum," said Kayne.

"What? You know the rules," said Josh.

"Yes I know, but I had to get more in with them. It's just what I had to do. Anyway, I was speaking to Kyle and told him that I needed a check done on my car 'cos I think it had been spotted by the local old bill. I told him that I have a mate whose missus has been bulk shoplifting from The Padmouth MegaMall and they may have clocked her registration as they drove away. She's never been caught and is bloody good at what she does, so she might have to change her car. He told me he trusted me and could get it done for £200. It cost £100 and he would take the other half of the £200 for himself. I asked him how he did it and he said that he had only been doing it for the last month and had a copper in his pocket who had given him a name and number who could do it for me. He said he could turn it around in a day so I could get rid of the car if I needed to. I said, look, I'd give him £400 there and then if he gave me the name of the person and the number, and I'd phone him myself. Kyle is greedy and said he would phone the person and get back to me. So I left, and about an hour later he phoned me and said that he had spoken to his bloke who agreed, and said that I could phone him this afternoon after 3pm; I've already paid him the £400. I've got a first name and number if you want it."

There was silence. Josh gulped and looked at Andy. "What you think?"

Andy pondered. "Well. You've committed a crime which is against the rules, but in the circumstances this'll probably be squared off with Martin. Yes, we'd better take it," he said to Josh.

"Go on, then," said Josh. "I don't know who I have to call, but I've got the number. I have to tell them that I'm a friend of Kyle and say that he said that it's okay for me to phone. Whoever it is trusts Kyle so there's no hassle with it. The number is..." Kayne picked up their phone from the table and scrolled through his contacts and said, "Here it is. It's 07890 324517. You give the person a registration and they will tell you when you are on the phone who owns it, who last checked it and if there is any interest in it. Afterwards I give the money to Kyle who meets the person and pays them. It's that bloody easy - and there is no chance of anyone getting caught. I know I've just said it, but it really *is* that easy. Simple."

"Really? That easy?" said Josh.

Andy chipped in. "I've seen this type of thing before. It's quite a common way of getting information from police systems. The trouble is a lot of this type of information is all talk and we rarely catch anyone, but for you to get the numbers like you've done is like gold dust. Fantastic. So you'll phone them this afternoon?"

"Yes," replied Kayne.

"Better get our skates on," said Andy. Unlike Josh, Andy had experienced this type of scenario before but not with this amount of detail. He was used to this kind of pressure whilst managing informants but was not a supervisor and knew they had to get the relevant authority to allow Kayne to lawfully do this. He started to take control of the meeting, as he knew Josh was feeling uncomfortable about how the whole situation was going.

"Right, this is what we do. You go home, sit tight and we'll phone and tell you what to do by 2pm. We'll get you your money back by the end of the week. "You got enough to pay Kyle if he asks for the money later?" he asked.

"Yes" said Kayne.

"Great. We'll let you know what registration we want you to get checked. Is that okay?"

"Sounds good to me; and I'll phone you back once I've done it, yeah?"

"Yep," said Andy. "Sorted. Right, anything else?"

Josh then said hurriedly and a bit nervously, "Don't commit crime, don't tell anyone what you are doing and don't set anyone else up..." he said to cover himself. "Yes. You say that every time. Don't bloody panic! It'll be fine," said Kayne. He picked up his phone that had been on the table and smiled. "I'm doing this for you boys. You might get promoted on the back of this, Josh," and smiled as he walked off.

Josh looked at Andy. "Blimey. What you think of that?" he said. "Great! Love this," Andy said. "Better get back and let Martin know. I'll phone Michelle and Helen and let them know that we can meet them back in the office." They got up from the table and walked out of the coffee shop.

Helen had been watching the front door of the coffee shop and saw Kayne come out of it by himself. She saw him walk back across the park towards his van. She got out of the Golf and followed him at slightly more of a distance than she had when he'd arrived so she would again not be spotted by him. She watched him approach his van and put his hand in his right tracksuit bottom pocket to get his keys. As he did so she saw a smartly dressed man rush around from the other side of the van and start shouting at Kayne. He was in his late 50s, bald and dressed in a dark coloured suit. At the same time he was shouting at Kayne; he was pointing at him; she saw him push him in the chest with some force, Kayne taking a step back to check his balance. He then took stock, regained his stance and stepped forward - but then, just suddenly stood still. He was staring straight ahead looking at the man. Kayne didn't look scared but was expressionless with a nonchalant look about him.

Helen carried on walking close by the two of them along the path back towards the supermarket, as she had to do in order to keep her cover. She could only hear a couple of things the man was saying to Kayne, like "you've been caught out this time" and "this is it. I've had enough of you fucking about." Helen continued on the path and made her way into the supermarket. She could see Michelle sitting in their car close to the entrance and could just about see the two men standing together. Helen found a safe place in the supermarket to phone Michelle. "It's me," she said. "Can you see what's happening?" "Yes," said Michelle. "Just stay on the phone and I'll talk you through it. The male in the suit is still pointing his finger at Kayne and...wait one...he's turned round and he's gone round the other side of the van...I can't see him now...oh yes...a car has just driven off at speed from the other side of the van . . . Kayne has got into the van . . which is just reversing . . .and is driving off at speed. You still there, Helen?" "Yep". "Do you want to come back to the car?" "Yep. Will do, give me a couple of minutes. I'll get us a can of pop each," said Helen, and a few minutes later walked back to where Michelle was sitting in their car. Helen gave a can to Michelle and opened hers. "Bloody hell. What happened there?" Michelle pondered, sipping from hers. "Looks like Kayne might have been rumbled," mused Helen. "Couldn't really hear too much, just saw a bloke shouting at Kayne and it didn't look too good. I'll phone Josh and let him know."

Josh and Andy were already in the unlocked Golf as they had agreed with Helen, and had driven off en route back to the office where they had arranged to meet up for a debrief. Andy had been driving only a few minutes when the hands-free phone went off in the car. "Guys, it's Helen. We've got a problem. I've seen Kayne being shouted at by a bloke in a suit who was waiting by the van when Kayne got back to it. He was having a right go at him. You might just want to put a call in to him Josh, to see what that was all about but it didn't look good." Josh turned pale. "Right," he agreed. "I'll do it now. Cheers." Josh turned to Andy. "Told you this wasn't a good move, looks like our luck's run out. Kayne is going to go bloody mad, I'll phone him now." Josh dialled Kayne's number. It rang and rang. There was no reply. "Bloody hell, answer it, Kayne, you tit!" exclaimed Josh. "I'll try again — come *on*! Bloody *answer*!" He rang Kayne again. Josh was panicking; he didn't need this. He needed Kayne, and the operation needed Kayne too. More importantly, Kayne didn't need the grief in being rumbled. Josh tried again. "What is it?" Kayne answered. "You Okay?" Josh asked. "Yep. Why?" said Kayne. "We just saw you having a barney with a bloke in a suit. You sure that you are alright?" "Ha! Of course" said Kayne. "That was my manager checking up on me. The van has a tracking device and he found me there. I've been here twice in two days and he wondered why as it's not on my normal route. He asked what I was doing there and I told him that I went into the supermarket to get a sandwich, then a decent coffee in the coffee shop. Don't panic. He warned me to get the work done or he'd give me the boot. To be honest I wouldn't mind if he did. Crap job and he's a knob." "Well, if that's the case and you don't mind getting the sack, we can always make sure we meet there next time!" breathed Josh, feeling a lot more relaxed. Andy scowled at Josh disapprovingly. He worried about Josh sometimes. He was too close and friendly with Kayne, and Andy felt it wasn't a healthy balance for the handler/informant relationship. "Yes mate. Please do," said Kayne. "Better shoot. I'm not hands free!" and laughed as the phone cut off. "He's getting bloody cocky" Andy said to Josh. "It'll all end in tears, mark my words." Josh looked at Andy. "He's on fire, great stuff. It'll be fine." Andy shook his head.

It had been an eventful meeting in terms of the tradecraft, with everyone doing their job to ensure each other was safe, albeit Kayne being rumbled for not being on his approved courier route by his boss; nonetheless, the type of information that Kayne had provided was valuable. Josh had never experienced the likes of this information before. He was nervously excited and wondered what would happen next.

Chapter 10

Martin had stayed in the office whilst the team went out to the meeting with Kayne, and Jim hadn't come back after his daily 9.30am meeting. Ellie had come into work late again just after 9am, and as a researcher was the engine room of the office; without her, the whole process of obtaining intelligence from the informants, through to disseminating to those who needed it would halt. She was single and had a bit of a party lifestyle. Yesterday was the excuse about the motorway traffic, today it might have been that she was stuck behind a dustcart. But Martin didn't really mind if she was a bit late. She understood the process by which the team met informants and dealt with all the issues that unfolded afterwards, and as long as she finished her work he was relaxed about the whole thing. She worked at her computer and let other departments have the intelligence the informants produced. It was quite a simple process but needed someone to do it who was very discreet as well as being completely efficient – and Ellie was both.

"Everything alright?" she enquired of Martin. "You seem a bit distant. Not your usual self." "Yes, thanks," he said. "Just thinking. Got a lot on at the moment." He looked at his watch; it was 11.36am. He knew Josh and Andy were meeting Kayne at 11am so they should be finished by now. He just hoped they'd get back before Jim turned up at the office and back to his desk. He thought it best if he phoned them and learned what had happened before they arrived. He phoned Andy as he knew he wouldn't be driving. "Hi. You on the way back?" "Yes" said Andy. "And?" "Well, it's like this. We've got the name of a copper and his mobile number who can do registration checks and get all the usual details like owner and who did the last check. Kayne's planning to phone him after 3pm today. It's already cost him £400 but we can sort that out for him, can't we?" "Andy! Hold on a minute. He's going way too far in getting that sort of information without all the authorities and everything that goes with it. I'll have to speak to the Anti-Corruption Unit and see what they say. You far away?" "30 minutes," was the reply. "Right. Get back here and don't type anything up just yet. Don't say anything to anyone and if Jim's here just say he gave you something about a bit of drug dealing and nothing else. Whatever happens, he can't know about this. I'll give you a bell once I know what the Anti-Corruption Team say." "Okay Sarge," Andy said. He loved the drama of these types of situations.

Martin made his excuses to Ellie and hurriedly left the office. He walked the short distance across the car park in the Headquarters complex and entered the Anti-Corruption Team building. He went quickly up two flights of steps and knocked on the door of Keith Catlin's office. "Come in," called Keith. Martin was a bit out of breath. "Boss. I've got an update for you," Martin began. "And I've got one for you, Martin. Take a seat," Keith replied.

Martin sat down again in the comfy chair in front of Keith's desk. "You first," said Keith. Martin then relayed to him the information that Andy had just told him. "Mmm. Looking a bit tasty, this one," Keith noted, adding, "What's your plan?" "Let's do it," said Martin.

"As long as you can give me the authority to get our person to put in a call, they'll do it this afternoon. We can then see who does the check and take it from there." "Authority granted at 11.50hrs," said Keith, making a note of the time in his daybook. "So this is what I've got," Keith went on. "I saw Jim yesterday afternoon and showed him the information about Dave Harrison. He just dismissed it and said that he (Harrison) would never do anything like that. That was about it, short and sweet, and then he left; I didn't tell him who had told us. To be honest, I was a bit taken aback. I mean if I were him, I'd declare that I knew Harrison and ask for someone else to get involved in assessing the information and possibly contacting the informant; it doesn't really feel right. If you ask me, we need to examine that sort of information further; what I need you to do is to get a meeting with Harrison's sister-in-law and get some more out of her. Don't tell Jim, and I'll get all the relevant authorities arranged for you by the ACC. Don't put anything on your systems and just get the handlers to write everything on paper, nothing to do with this typed on any computers. You agreeable with all that? It's a lot of pressure but I'm sure you and the team are up to it." Martin took a deep breath. "Okay" he said slowly, "so long as the team are looked after properly and all the authorities are sorted and everything's written down. I don't want anyone coming in left field when this is all done and dusted and start criticising any of us for what we've done. This is proper covert stuff, and I know when there is any enquiry all the technical stuff gets scrutinised with a fine tooth-comb." "Listen, Martin," said Keith. "There is no other way of catching these bastards. They're a scourge on this force and no one is going to criticise either you, the team, or me if you are doing things to find the cause of this. Guaranteed top cover for you and the guys." "Right," said Martin. "Game on. I'll phone you once we get a call put in and let you know what happens." Martin got up from the comfy chair and walked towards the door. He turned and spoke to Keith. "Love this, boss. Just like to get these bent bastards; it makes all the hassle worthwhile. And we'll get them, trust me." Keith smiled. "Me too. We'll get them," he concurred.

Martin left the Anti-Corruption Unit building and walked back towards his office. It was lunchtime and he decided to go the canteen to get something to eat and work out his next move. He phoned Andy. "You two back yet?" he asked. "We're just getting back into the car park. You need anything?" Andy replied. "Can you two meet me in the canteen and get Michelle and Helen to see me in there too, please? I've got an update for you all." "Sure, Sarge. See you in five minutes."

Martin carried on walking towards the canteen. He knew that the work the team was carrying out was something over and above what they were used to. Michelle, Andy and Helen had dealt with informants who had provided intelligence about corruption within the force before, but not in the same team with two informants at the same time. The timing seemed strange and possibly coincidental, but he would not let himself be drawn into thinking they were one and the same, and that they might be linked. More often, you would get information about corruption that came along once every three or four months, and only rarely did it come to anything that could be proven. He knew not only had *he* to ensure that Jim did not know what was going on with the team and the information was kept away from his gaze, but he also had to ensure that the team appeared gainfully employed running informants. It was a conundrum, but he relished the challenge. As long as Keith was true to his word and he and the team had top cover over and above Jim, then their reputation and job would be safe.

Martin went into the canteen. He bought a cup of tea and found a table in the corner of the room, well away from where people were sitting. It was nearing lunchtime and he knew the canteen would soon start filling up and become noisy. A few minutes later Josh and Andy came into the room and joined him. Helen and Michelle soon followed; they all sat around the table. "Right guys. Sorry to have dragged you all down here, but I've got something to tell you all that mustn't go any further — and I mean *no* further. The Anti-Corruption team received some information yesterday that relates to a PC from Padmouth, Dave Harrison. Allegedly, he is passing confidential information to his brother. The informant is a female relative calling herself 'Susan'. This is a fantastic chance to get him, Harrison, finally. He's rumoured to have been at it for a few years but nothing has ever come of it. This could be our only real and best chance to get him. This job is for you two." Martin looked at Michelle and Helen. "Fine," agreed Helen. "When do you want us to call her?" "This afternoon, please," said Martin. "This needs to be progressed ASAP. I'll give you all her details upstairs in the office. Josh, I've spoken to Keith Catlin in the Anti-Corruption Unit. He's given the green light to Kayne being able to get the registration check done this afternoon. If you can phone him and say that he's good to go, then we will see what happens. Could you ask him to get our team's VW Golf checked, it's on its covert number plates so any result will come back to the covert business and not arouse any suspicion. We can then see who does any check on it. Arrange to meet him again tomorrow and give him £500. That's £400 he paid Kyle for the check and £100 for doing it." "Only £100?" Josh put in. "That's a bit tight, Sarge." "Okay, give him £200 and then there might be a bit more for any result that comes of it." "Nice one. Thanks," said Josh. "So everyone's cool and knows what they're doing?" Martin enquired. Everyone nodded. "Oh and another thing. Don't enter anything into the computer. If the boss asks, just say that tomorrow you and Helen are meeting with Ambrose Wilks that was meant to be today, but you had to change it 'cos of Josh's meeting today with Kayne, and then go on to meet this new informant before coming back to the office; and Josh...just say that Kayne...God... you can't say that you are meeting him three times in three days! Got any suggestions?" "Um...what about we don't tell Jim that we are meeting him at all, and just go out? Michelle and Helen can't do the cover as they have now got a meeting, so...I'll just say I've got to cover Michelle's meeting with Wilks," Josh proposed. "Blimey. It's all getting a bit tight." Martin agreed. "Listen. That's the best plan there is, unless anyone can think of anything better ...?" Nobody said anything. Just then, out of the corner of his eye, Martin saw Jim come into the canteen. He was by himself and went to get a can of drink from the chill cabinet. He was wearing his normal dour expression. "Oi, oi," Martin hissed. "Watch out, the boss is about!" Jim paid for his can and saw his team having a catch up. His face broke into a somewhat forced laugh when he saw them and briefly started chatting with someone he knew sitting at another table in the canteen. They had a short conversation before he walked over to the table where the CO15 team were sitting. "Everyone alright"? he asked. "All good, Sir," said Martin. "Josh will tell you what happened this morning when we're back in the office." "Good, sounds interesting," said Jim. "How long you all been in here?" "Not long," answered Michelle. "Just having a break from the office and we'll be back in a mo." Jim glared at her and his mood suddenly changed. "Another ten minutes and I'll see you lot in the office. You really haven't got time to be spending in here gassing," he said.

With that, Jim turned and walked out of the canteen with his can of drink. "He's not happy" Andy observed to Martin. "Can't work him out. He can be nice as pie to his so-called mates, and like, bloody rude to us; there's no reason for it. I'm beginning to like him a bit less every day he stays as the boss." Josh chipped in, "If they can promote that idiot to a DI there's hope for you yet Martin! If *he* can get paid for being a manager, any idiot can do it!" Martin laughed. "Look. I'm not interested in getting promoted, I just want this team to prove its' worth. There's a lot of experience in this team and it can easily deal with his ridiculous nonsense. We just have to stick together and get to the bottom of this corruption stuff. Just keep it tight and don't tell anyone about what's going on. I mean, this is no joke. If it gets out that we are talking stuff about corruption without Jim knowing, I'll definitely be for the high-jump. I've got a feeling he doesn't want me in the team and wants to put his own person in. Just a gut feeling I've got and maybe I'm right who knows, perhaps one day I'll possibly be proved right." He hadn't told the team or anyone about Jim's comments to him the day before about him paying for something. He hadn't dwelt on it, but it was at the back of his mind as Jim's way of trying to make him leave voluntarily. Besides, he had to see these two corruption jobs through and it was impossible for him to leave the team in the short term. These sorts of enquiries didn't come round very often, and it was unusual to have two to manage at once; the team needed support and he had to stay to give it.

They finished their drinks and started to get up from the table knowing they couldn't be too long before they had to be back in the office and see what the afternoon would bring.

Chapter 11

Paul Slacke wasn't the most productive officer Dorshire Police had ever employed. He had reached the rank of Sergeant by the time he had given fourteen years of service and had been stuck there ever since. He'd been employed on various teams around the force without ever making a name for himself. He was one of those officers who had managed somehow to get the jobs that didn't really bring on too much stress. It was not what anyone from the outside looking in would describe as a glittering career. He was also one of those people who knew the right folk to get where he wanted; he was an outspoken character and not scared to have his voice heard. In fact, he was one of the most vociferous of the Police Federation representatives the force had had for a long time. He knew the police rules and regulations backwards and over the years it had stood him in good stead. He'd had his brushes with the Anti-Corruption Unit like most officers had over the course of their careers, but because of this, he had decided to fight fire with fire. He became involved with helping his colleagues when it came to disciplinary issues, he was someone therefore you would want on your side if you were ever in trouble with the job, as he knew how to play the system. If he had spent less time studying the rulebook and more time on proper policing, then it would be fair to say that he would have earned his pay.

The job he was in currently suited Paul well. It was a 9am-5pm Monday to Friday routine with weekends off. This fitted in with his lifestyle and domestic arrangements. His bitter and protracted divorce was a long time ago with the arrangement being, he saw his two teenage children every other weekend. Partly due to his divorce, money was tight as he had maintenance to pay for his teenagers. He rented a one bedroom flat in Padmouth and lived the divorced, single-bloke lifestyle that a few of his acquaintances had drifted back to, once their marriages had broken down. Not working shifts suited him well as he could get himself down the pub most evenings, and this is where he did most of his socialising. In fact, his drinking had become progressively worse over the years and at one point he'd been caught drink driving and was arrested and charged. By managing to pull a few strings, he had received a sanction from the force but whether it was luck, coincidence or both, he hadn't lost his job. His drinking habit had led to the breakdown of his marriage and despite this, hadn't gotten to grips with his excesses, in fact it had deteriorated. Paul didn't have much going for him; like Jim, he was a bit of a loner with few friends. It wasn't that he enjoyed being alone, he was just one of those people that no one wanted to befriend. He had just over 29 years in the police and consequently wasn't seeking promotion or a change of roles. This job as the Sergeant in the Traffic Process Unit would see him just fine until he could retire; which was little under a year away. He had several civilian members of staff to manage, but they were no problem at all and just got on with their work.

Having the Dorshire Police Traffic Process Unit was a plum job for Paul. The trouble was like many plum jobs across the force it was under scrutiny from the cost-cutters and bean counters. His post was one of those under consideration for civilianisation and therefore cheaper; and why wouldn't it be? Why did the force need a warranted officer on a sergeant's wage doing the role, when a civilian at half the cost could do the same job. To be honest, a civilian could have carried it out far better than Paul. For several months he had been worried about the next round of cuts and he needed a Plan B. Paul was well-connected around the force and knew he would be able to find someone, somewhere, he could persuade to be on his side. He had been speaking to a few of his colleagues around the force and they all knew he was looking for an escape route.

In the early afternoon on Tuesday, he heard a knock on his office door. "Come in," he barked with a gruff Irish accent. The handle turned, and the door opened. It was Jim. "Ha! You don't normally knock. Come in and sit down. What is it?" he asked. Jim didn't look best pleased; in fact he was fuming. Paul could see the anger etched in his face. "It's my bloody CO15 team. They are all nothing but a bunch of bloody prima-donnas. Ever since I went there a few weeks ago we haven't gotten on. What they don't bloody like is me saying no to them. To be honest I don't think they are used to it. I think that for too long they have been running the ship. Well, when I say *they*, I mean Martin. Thinks he knows everything and forgets that I'm in charge. He is a typical jumped-up little Sergeant who thinks that he knows best and pays lip service to anything that I say. It's like he thinks that because he has been involved with informants so long, what I say doesn't wash with him. With more cuts coming they, and Martin in particular, had better watch out 'cos I won't stand for any more of their ruddy nonsense." Before Paul had a chance to say anything Jim continued in his forceful, agitated and aggressive manner. "Look. I've got a plan that I just need you to have a think about. I need help in getting rid of Martin, like moving him on. If I did that, I won't have any trouble with the powers that be, and if I get him to go voluntarily it'll be a hell of a lot easier. The team are right behind him and without him, they'll be easy to manage. So it's like this. If I can get Martin out, how do you fancy doing his role? We can get things sorted, if you know what I mean."

There was a bit of a pause. Paul looked at Jim. "But if I said yes, how are you going to do that? Like, get me in that team as a skipper with no experience. I haven't even got that long until I retire." "Easy," said Jim. "Operational need and I'm the boss, so I can say what goes. No one really gives a flying stuff about covert policing now; they don't care. It's all about cost-cutting and no one would want that role. There's no one out there with the experience, and who would want to do it, so it would be a case of getting in there and learning on the job. I'll look after you and then it would be a case of the rest would go gradually and I'd get those in the team that I want in there. Look, eventually the unit will be totally cut, but no one knows that yet. I can say when it goes and make it as good or bad as I want. I'll play them and make it that bad for them that they won't want to stay. C'mon. What you say? It's easy."

Paul sat back in his chair and took a deep breath. He knew that to get him the job in CO15 would be something of tall order for Jim to pull off. It would start tongues wagging around Headquarters and around the force too. "You sure? I mean someone's going to say it's like having a square peg in a round hole and all that..." Jim cut across him. He had a bad habit of doing this with everyone, not just Paul. "Listen Paul. I've done it before and I'll do it again; it'll be fine. You in? I haven't got the time to be waiting around for an answer." Paul pondered. "If you say so, it's a yes, but it better not backfire and I end up sent to custody or section. Same hours?" "Yep. Keep the faith" said Jim. "Trust me. I haven't let you down yet over the years and don't intend to now." Right! Done" agreed Paul. "Just let me know when you want me to start and I'll tie up a few things this end." "Great," replied Jim. "I'll give you a bell in a couple of days."

Paul smiled ruefully; he winked at Jim as he got up. They shook hands and Jim walked towards the door. As Jim left, Paul added, "Won't let you down." "You know," said Jim, "and open the bloody window, I can smell whisky or something in here; it must be from you going out last night, eh?" Paul smiled but ignored him and went to open the window.

Jim left Paul's office and made his way across the car park, back towards the CO15 office. He knew he had Paul exactly where he wanted him; this had been the case for a few years. Paul hadn't and would not change, but he was stuck in a rut in life and needed to keep his working hours. Jim knew Paul was looking for another job that suited his lifestyle, and Jim was the man who would make this happen - he would do anything to get what he wanted. The CO15 team was increasingly irritating him and he decided he had to act by first getting rid of Martin.

In the time it had taken for Jim to visit Paul, the CO15 team had returned to the office and set about getting on with their work. The handlers were busy typing their records but were very conscious the boss could walk in at any time. Michelle had spoken to her new informant and had arranged to meet her the next day. Josh had called Kayne and given him the details of the team's covert VW Golf that he wanted checked on the computer. Kayne was worldly wise and no mug and had already cleared with Josh how much he was going to be paid for doing this task.

Martin was very conscious of the work he had asked his team to do behind Jim's back. It was a high-risk strategy, but one which Martin knew he could pull off if he had the continued support of his team and they could all hold their nerve. It normally all ended with a positive result and the Anti-Corruption Unit happy with the outcome. Informants didn't tend to be wrong when it came to reporting on corruption issues.

The team were busy typing when they heard the familiar squeak of the floorboards as someone approached the office door. They all knew who it would be, and in a couple of seconds Jim walked in. Martin looked up from his desk, whereas the others continued typing. "Hiya boss," said Martin. "Everything alright"? Jim looked down at him. "I've had better days. Can you pop in my office in ten minutes please? I've just got a call to make. I'll let you know when I'm done." "Sure," agreed Martin. Jim walked into his office and closed the door. The team looked up from their keyboards and looked knowingly at each other. They had heard what Jim had said to Martin and felt for him; they knew that he was under a lot of pressure and hoped that Jim hadn't worked out what was going on behind his back.

It wasn't long before Jim called Martin into his office. Martin got up from his chair and walked into Jim's office. "Close the door,

Martin." Martin did as directed and sat down. Jim lowered the volume of his voice in case the team were listening. "Look, Martin. I'm going to be quite blunt with you. There's obviously something going on with the team that they don't like since I started here, and I don't like atmospheres in an office. It's a small, close-knit team and we all need to get on. I'm a different sort of boss from Dan, and what you are all, and you in particular are used to. Dan really let you get on and run the team in your own way but I'm a bit more intrusive in terms of how I manage things. You've probably noticed that I'm very direct and won't tolerate time-wasting informants or lazy handlers. Things have really got to change in the next week or so or I'm going to have to get things moving for you. That means a change of attitude in the team towards me, and if they don't, I'll hold you responsible. You are in charge daily about how they perform and how productive they are. It's not professional on their part for them to be anything but the best, and you are their supervisor; it's down to you and you alone. If this role is no longer for you, just let me know and I can arrange a move away from CO15 for you." There was a pause. Jim stared at Martin with an expressionless face. Is there anything you want to say?" he asked.

Martin sat there in disbelief and in stunned silence. He looked at Jim, not quite knowing what to say. "Sir. I have listened to what you have to say, but there is nothing I can do to change what they are doing. They are a great team who are working very hard in a difficult climate. The cuts are hanging over them, but I will try my very best as ever to get them to engage with you in a more..." Jim chipped in, "Respectful way, please." Martin nodded. "Yes. I suppose so. A respectful way." Jim then said, "Martin. I'll give you a week, and if there's no difference in their attitude and productivity, then it'll be *you* not them moving jobs." Martin looked at Jim again. He had learned exactly what Jim was like in the time he had been the boss, and he meant what he said, in that he had a week to turn things around. He also knew Jim was well-connected in the force, and if he wanted to move him he would be moved. The issues of fairness and getting Human Resources involved would be futile, as Jim would just bypass the normal ways things should be done in the force. Jim was old school, and Martin knew Jim would, and could, get around systems as he had done all his career. Martin was very much against that old style regime but knew it still went on in certain cliques, and at the same time knew that he couldn't do anything at all about it; he was effectively stuck. Martin also remembered what Jim had said to him the day before. It was an old-school way of doing things which unfortunately still went on in certain quarters. Martin wasn't daft and suspected that Jim was planning to get rid of him, either him going voluntarily, or by him being pushed. Martin was determined that neither of these alternatives would happen. This was just the beginning of a battle of wills. A clash of wills that Jim was determined would have only one result, and that Martin was equally determined would have another. For Martin, rank didn't come into it.

"Anything else to say, Martin?" "No, Sir. That's it then, ta." Martin just sat there and looked at Jim. "One more thing," Jim went on. "I've got the report for the Surveillance Commissioner to do tomorrow so if I'm not in and anyone asks, I'm probably going to be working from home. She's coming to do the inspection on Monday, so it gives me just a few days to get it all together. Dan didn't do much of it as he was leaving, so I'm struggling a bit and need to complete it a bit pronto. Don't suppose there is anything you can do on it for me?" There was a tinge of sarcasm in his voice. Martin just sat there. There was plenty he could do to help, but with everything Jim had said to him, he was not in any way inclined to help him out. "No, Sir" he said curtly. "Nothing."

Martin got up and left Jim's office, closing the door behind him with a bit more of a tug than he would usually have done. The team glanced up at him from their keyboards as they heard the door hit the frame with some force. Martin sat down at his desk and started typing. He wasn't really paying much attention to what he was doing. He knew he wanted to tell the team what was going on but needed to keep the politics happening between him and Jim away from them. They had enough on their plates with the corruption jobs that were rumbling on, without having to worry about all the silliness the boss was engineering. All he knew was that nobody or nothing would take him away from the job he had been in for nearly fifteen years, and no attempt at bullying by Jim would force on him his narrow-minded views on informant handling, and oversee the demise of him and the CO15 team; not when there was so much work still to be done.

Chapter 12

It was the end of the working day; 4pm had come and gone and Martin was on his way home. The drive from work to his house wasn't that far but he very often became stuck in traffic. He left work just after the schools in that area of town had finished for the day, and his route was inevitably congested with school children making their way home, made worse by parents collecting them in their cars. Martin was normally very good at switching off from work. He had been in the role for so many years, he had devised a technique that meant when he reached a certain place like a road sign or house, he would force himself not to think about work. It was a technique he had told his teams about and they had adopted it too. It just meant that it was a way of escaping from work even though his phone could go off at any time. However, he would almost certainly be called sometime in the evening or during the night.

Tonight was no exception. He had only been away from the office for twenty minutes and had just driven past the road sign he used for switching off from work, when the inevitable happened. It was earlier than usual when the handsfree phone in the car kicked in and he answered. "Hello, who's that?"

"Sarge. It's Josh. You free to speak?"

"Yes mate" said Martin. "What's up?"

"I've just had a call from Kayne. He's put a call in to the man to get the check done and he's got it all sorted with the details about who owns the car. He did it in a flash. It's all a bit strange." Josh sounded worried.

"Go on. What is it?" said Martin. "Well. Kayne phoned the man like he said he would and gave him the registration of the car. The bloke said wait on the phone for a few minutes which he did, and then he told him who owned it. It was that easy."

"And?" Martin didn't really know where the conversation was going. "Does this really need to be told to me right this minute? I'm driving." Martin wasn't best pleased with getting this type of information off-duty. It wasn't really time critical and could have waited until the morning. There was a bit of a silence on the phone. "You still there?" asked Martin.

"Yes, yes," said Josh.

"And?"

"The details Josh gave for the car goes down to our VW Golf that's registered to our covert company, and although he didn't get the name of the bloke who did the check he said he had a local accent."

There was a pause. Martin gulped. His heart started racing. "You sure"? he gasped.

"Yep. Straight up," said Josh.

"Bloody hell. So how's Kayne left it with him?" asked Martin.

"That's it. Got the check done and he'll pay Kyle. It's as straightforward as that."

"Is he alright"? Martin asked.

"Yep, all good. No questions asked. I've arranged to meet him tomorrow to give him his money; you okay with that?"

Martin had by now pulled over into a side road to try to take stock and work out what he was going to do. "Um. Yep. He got the information like we asked him to and of course we'll pay him. I'm going to have to square things off with the Anti-Corruption Unit first thing tomorrow and see where we go from there. What time are you meeting him?"

"11am at the usual place," said Josh.

"Good work. Well done. I'll see you first thing in the office." "Great".

He pressed the red button that was on his steering wheel to disconnect the call; Martin took a deep breath. There might be a few people with a local accent who could have made that check, so what he had now didn't narrow it down very much. Coming up with the check on the car that was the team's covert company as a result, would not have aroused any suspicion; the check was being done on an *unmarked* covert police vehicle. This was a clever ploy by Martin and a check of the records would show when and where it was done and by whom; the results would be really interesting.

Martin pondered as he sat in the car. He reached for his phone and starting texting Keith. "Evening, Sir. Got some interesting information for you. Can wait until tomorrow. I'll come over and see you about 8.30am. Cheers. Martin." The reply came back almost immediately. "Okay." Martin smiled to himself. Something was amiss, but this was a great chance to get to the bottom of it. If he continued to have Keith on his side, things would work out just fine.

Chapter 13

It was Wednesday morning and the team assembled in the office as they did to start the day - every day. It hadn't been a great week so far and the team remained subdued; Martin was on edge. He knew the corruption job Josh was dealing with was gathering pace, and now they had been given checkable facts the situation had more credence. The check on the covert VW Golf number plate needed to be done that morning, and Josh had to meet his informant to give him his reward money. Michelle and Helen were going out to meet their new informant 'Susan' and this also required managing very carefully. Martin was normally quite a calm person, but he could feel his stress levels rising.

At 8.20am he called the team together for the daily office meeting. Although Jim said he probably wasn't coming into the office because he was working from home that day, there was still a chance he might turn up. Martin was on edge. "Morning all. Right. We've got a lot on now and there isn't much time to waste. Just to go through a few things before we get going for the day. Josh...you're meeting Kayne at 11 with Andy?" "Yes, Sarge," he said. "Usual place but I ain't got any cover 'cos Michelle and Helen are meeting their new informant." "That's fine. Just make sure you do a proper route and you don't get compromised." Josh was somewhat put out. "Never have and never will," he muttered. Andy looked at Josh but didn't say anything. "And

Michelle and Helen. You two alright to meet 'Susan' or whatever her real name turns out to be?" "Yes, Sarge. All sorted to meet just outside Padmouth in the foyer of the Holiday Go Hotel. We've used the route she'll go through a few times before, so there are no worries there. It's a good one." "Great" said Martin. "I'm happy with that. I just need everyone to remember that nothing is to be said to the boss, whatever happens from either of the sources that are talking about the two jobs we have on now." The team could hear the seriousness in Martin's voice and knew that he meant it. "It really is *very* important that we don't reveal anything to anyone; *everything* comes through me; I can't stress that enough. I know it is tough at the minute for everyone, but we must stick together, and we'll get through this." You could feel the tension in the room. To have one corruption job running was tough but to have two just increased the stress. "You okay, Sarge?" asked Helen. She could tell he was under pressure. "Yes thanks. I've just got a lot on at the moment; plenty to think about, but thanks for asking." Helen had encountered stress in a previous supervisor and seen how it could all go wrong, with her having to take a long time off work. Helen didn't want to see Martin away with the same issues. "Right guys. Give me a call when you are all done and safe and sound. I've got to pop over to the Anti-Corruption Unit now and give them an update. It seems like I'm spending a lot of my time over there nowadays. But that's no problem. All good." He smiled and picked up his mobile phone and left the office in a hurry.

The team gathered their things together and chatted before they left to go to their respective meetings. "What do you make of Martin today?" asked Andy. "He looks like he's a bit stressed, but I'm not surprised," Josh replied. "He's got a lot on and doesn't seem to be getting much support from that miserable sod that is Jim. I mean, Jim doesn't know what the sources are talking about and Martin's probably thinking that he'll sack the sources if they don't look as if they're providing anything. I wouldn't want to be in Martin's shoes. We just have to make sure he doesn't go 'pop' and give him as much support as we can." Michelle piped up. "I'll make a cake tonight and bring it in tomorrow. He loves Victoria Sponge; and cake is the answer to every problem in the world!" They all laughed and made their way out of the office.

Martin left his office and walked purposefully across the car park towards the Anti-Corruption Unit building. As he did so he passed the canteen and could see Paul Slacke in there by himself. He was hunched over the table and looked as if he was texting someone. Martin decided it was best not to speak to him; Martin was a man on a mission. He hadn't slept very well for the last few nights what with the comments from Jim, along with the fact that he was managing informants providing information about corruption behind his boss' back. But now that he had some checkable information to give to Keith, it seemed that the hassle was a little bit more worthwhile. He hadn't heard from Jim during the morning, even to phoning in to check how things were, so that was a good thing in his book. Not to hear from Jim at all was a bonus; he presumed Jim was working from home. Martin hadn't put it past Jim, that this was just another check he would do to see what the team was up to.

Martin concluded Jim wasn't that clever, and any excuse to get away from the office Jim would take. Martin wasn't alone in thinking that working from home meant being at home minus the work and still getting paid.

Martin reached the Anti-Corruption Unit and entered the building. He went up the stairs and knocked on Keith's door. "Come in." Martin walked in. "Morning, guv, you okay"? "Yes, Martin. Take a seat." Martin sat down in the beige comfy chair. It was nice to be in an environment where he was working with a boss who was on his side, something he wasn't getting from his immediate boss, Jim. "So, what you got?" enquired Keith. Martin took a deep breath and, unusually for him was a bit nervous. Maybe it was to do with the fact that he enjoyed giving some juicy intelligence to the Anti-Corruption Unit. It was this type of work that he relished and made all the hassle worthwhile. "Well; we've got a mobile number that our person called to get a check done on a car. We had it done on our covert VW Golf and the results came back straight away. We're meeting our friendly informant this morning to pay them out, and we'll get the exact details of who owns the car and all that stuff. It would be handy to find out who did the check as we weren't given those details".

Martin slid a piece of paper with the details on it across the desk to Keith. Keith looked at them. "Interesting. Wait a minute and I'll get some checks done on the reg." He picked up the phone and called DC Rob Boakes. "Rob. Can you pop up to my office, please?" A minute later Rob appeared. "Can you do some checks on this number and reg please, like who the phone number goes down to and who last did a check on the reg; and I need the details ASAP. Cheers." Rob took the piece of paper Martin had written on and disappeared out of Keith's office. "Very interesting" he said to Martin. "Are you getting any more? We could do with a bit of a leg up with this job." "Yes, boss. We've got a meeting this morning with

'Susan' or whatever her real name turns out to be. I've got a good feeling about her; there's just something not quite right about the whole thing. You know when you feel something in your water?" "Like what?" queried Keith. "Are you saying that the two jobs are connected?" "Don't know," said Martin. "It's just that there's a bad feeling in the office at the moment towards Jim, and these two jobs have come along at once. There's nothing connecting the two jobs with him, but it's just the timing of it all."

Keith looked at Martin. "You know something that I don't?" asked Keith. Martin looked back at him and paused slightly, making Keith a little bit anxious. Martin continued. "No. Just a feeling." Keith wasn't completely convinced but went along with what Martin said. "Yes, you might be right, but there's nothing linking them so far, and these things have a habit of coming along like the proverbial bus. It'll be interesting to see the results of the checks. I'll give you a call later when Rob gets back to me." "Sure thing, I'll wait to hear from you."

Martin stood up and walked towards the door. "Look forward to your call, boss. You just can't beat a well-placed informant to get a job moving along." He smiled and left the room. Keith pondered. He knew Martin was a very experienced officer, but so was he. You can't kid a kidder, and he had a gut feeling that Martin was holding back on telling him the whole truth. What was it he thought, what could it possibly be? Keith was an experienced interviewer, and he'd come across hardened criminals who were better liars than Martin.

Martin left the Anti-Corruption Unit building and walked across towards his office. He had to pass the entrance to the canteen and glanced in as he did so. He could see Paul Slacke was still on his phone and looked like he was still texting someone. He didn't really know Paul, but decided to have conversation with him to see if he could confirm whether he knew if Jim was coming into work that day or not.

Martin walked up to the table where Paul was sitting. "Morning, Paul. You okay?" "Morning. Yes, and you?" he enquired. "All fine with me, thanks. Do you know where Jim is today? He said he might be working from home." "I've just texted him as he's not here, so I presume he is," said Paul. "Not a bad job if you can get it, all this working from home." Martin smiled. "Ha! Could do with a bit of that myself." Paul paused for a moment. His phone beeped. He looked at his phone and started texting a reply. "Are you planning to move on at any time? It's just that I've heard a rumour that you might be," Paul said as he texted, not looking at Martin. Martin was taken aback. "From who?" he asked. "Not for me to reveal my sources," Paul replied. Martin looked at him. "You need to get some better sources." Paul carried on texting. Martin made his excuses and left the canteen. Although he didn't normally talk to him, Paul had proven himself to be the stirring idiot Martin always knew he was, and rude too. But although Paul's reputation went before him he did have his uses sometimes, and this was one of them. Martin now knew that Jim wasn't around all day. Whatever unfolded from the two meetings his team were having, it would make it easier for him to deal with the outcomes, whatever they might be.

Chapter 14

Michelle and Helen were en route to their meeting with 'Susan'. They had planned what was going to happen well in advance and so this was a well-rehearsed routine. They were a good double-act and knew how each other worked. They bounced off each other during informant debriefs like they were tag conversationalists.

They too were meeting their informant at 11am and would use a similar method of deploying their tradecraft. Michelle was meticulous with her planning and had given clear instructions to 'Susan' the day before. She had also found out what she looked like, as well as the colour and make of the car she would be driving.

The plan was that 'Susan' was going to park her car close to the hotel in a burger chain restaurant car park. She would wait there until Helen had seen her arrive and given the all-clear to Michelle if she thought that 'Susan' was by herself and wasn't being followed. After that Michelle would then call 'Susan' and tell her to walk into the burger restaurant, walk to the washroom and wash her hands in the sink that was furthest from the door. They knew the venue well and this had worked successfully as a method of identifying a new informant in the past. Helen would then go in too and introduce herself; after that the two would walk together out of the restaurant, across the road and into the foyer of Hotel

Go. Michelle had already booked a meeting room in the name of their covert company, and the meeting with 'Susan' would then go ahead. Everyone would be nice and safe, and the debrief could take place securely and without interruption.

They arrived at the Hotel Go at 10.40am. They parked their car in the hotel car park as planned and went their separate ways, Helen going to the restaurant and Michelle into the hotel. Helen got herself a coffee and sat at a table next to the window in the restaurant. She had a good view of the car park entrance. Like clockwork 'Susan' arrived at 11am on the dot, and just as she had told Michelle the day before, she was driving a dirty small brown Peugeot. The car had seen better days.

Helen didn't see anybody else in the car with her, or anyone who had obviously driven in behind her as if they were following her. She watched 'Susan' get out of her car and lock it, walk across the car park into the restaurant and wait a second as she let someone out before going into the washroom.

Helen called Michelle, and the rest of the plan then took effect. Helen walked into the washroom; there was no one else in there. She saw 'Susan' washing her hands in the sink furthest from the door and walked up next to her before starting to wash her hands too. There was a bit of a pause. "Hi. Susan?" ventured Helen as the two washed their hands. 'Susan' looked at her nervously. "Yes," was the timid reply. Helen was a great handler and immediately put her at ease by explaining to her what they would then do. "Just walk with me and act normally. You'll be fine 'Susan'" she assured her. Nothing else was said; 'Susan' just nodded and they left the restaurant together. It was all going well and there were no dramas before they reached the hotel foyer. So far so good, thought Helen.

Michelle was waiting patiently in the meeting room for the arrival of Helen and 'Susan'. A few minutes later there was a knock on the door; Michelle got up from her chair and opened it. The hotel meeting room was a converted bedroom where they had basically taken out the bed and replaced it with a long wooden table. The management had decided to furnish the rest of the room with six black leather clad business chairs that had been pushed in around it. In the middle of the table was a bottle of mineral water with four glasses, and a small bowl of individually wrapped mints. They had endeavoured to make it appear corporate but had unfortunately failed.

"Come in. Nice to meet you, 'Susan'. I'm Michelle and this is Helen. How are you feeling?" "Very nervous," said 'Susan'. "Well, listen pet. Take a seat and we will explain everything." 'Susan' sat down at the first chair she saw at the far end of the table so she was facing the door. Michelle locked the door. "There's no need to be nervous. I've been doing this sort of thing for a long time and it always ends up fine, so please don't worry. It's easy for me to say that I know, but you just must trust me. So alright, let's get a few things clear before we move on. You must tell me everything you know in its' fullest detail so I can assess it properly and we can make it work. You'll be perfectly safe if you listen carefully to the instructions, which are, don't commit crime, don't tell anyone what you are doing and don't set anyone up. Got it?" Michelle had gone off like a steam train with her giving instructions to 'Susan' as she had a habit of talking a lot. Susan looked at her wide-eyed, taking it all in. She was nervous but at the same time astute. "Yes, it's all very clear," said 'Susan'. "So, first things first. Who are you really, like *really*?" asked Michelle. Michelle didn't hang around with her questions. This is what her informants liked about her. She was straight to the point. There was no time to waste. 'Susan' looked at her. "You're good, aren't you?" she said. "Been doing it a long time," Michelle repeated, and smiled. 'Susan' smiled back looking at Michelle with knowing eyes. 'Susan' was in her early twenties but had that look of someone who knew a lot about life. One of those people you occasionally come across, and although they don't appear to be overly well educated or well off, they are just one of those switched-on cookies. She was dressed in a light grey tracksuit and a pair of shiny dark blue trainers. Her bleached blonde hair needed a bit of touching up as the roots had started showing and she had a small tattoo of a snake on the top of her right hand. "Okay. My real name is Amy; I'm the half-sister of Dave Harrison. I don't know if you know him, but he's in uniform around here in Padmouth. I just wanted to give you a fake name in case I wasn't going to be listened to. But I trust you and Helen; you both seem really nice." "We are," averred Helen as she smiled at Amy. "So, what do you know?" asked Michelle. Amy paused. "Well. It's like this," she said. "I'm the half-sister of Dave and our older brother who is called Mick. I'm the youngest by miles 'cos my mum remarried. Me and my brothers, as I call them, are really tight; we're family, they look after me. My mum's first husband was a fireman, but he left my mum when Dave and Mick were really young. I don't know what happened to my mum's first husband. He's not around anymore and my brothers don't see him; but my real dad's a wrong-un and my mum can't get away from him. She met him in the pub when she was on the rebound from her ex and she's stuck; I came along a few years after they got together. Me and my brothers grew up in Padmouth and know a lot of people. Most are good, and some are bad, but Mick is one of the bad ones and knows a lot of the bad ones too." "What are they into?" asked Helen. "Well, all sorts, really," said Amy. "Drugs mainly, 'cos that's where the money is. They've done it for years, but as they've got more and more money they've started getting involved with guns, and that's not funny now. Like they've started threatening people, and although I haven't seen one being shot, people have told me that they've used them in Bluebell Woods." "So you've seen them then?" asked Helen excitedly. "Yeh, but not being shot, just in the house, Mick's house; he has two, a long one and a black pistol thing. I don't really know." Although Amy had great information Michelle knew that this debrief was going to be hard work; but she was a patient soul and knew it took all sorts in life. There was no point in managing an articulate informant who knew very little. These were the sorts of challenges she really enjoyed.

"So, Amy. Do you know how long they've had the guns for, and like where Mick got them from?" Michelle asked. "Not really, but I think a few weeks. He got them from someone who lives abroad and who got them into the country. Someone who has a yacht in the marina; but I don't know who that is - sorry." "Don't apologise. It's great stuff that you're telling us," Michelle assured her. "Oh, I'm glad. Don't want to waste your time," said Amy. "Not at all," replied Michelle. "And anyway, why do you want to tell us all this? Like, what's your motivation?" Amy paused. "Can I be really honest with you both?" "Of course. That's what we are here for," Helen answered. "Well, it's a couple of things really. I don't want Mick getting caught with guns 'cos he'll get sent down for a long time. The drugs you'll never catch him with 'cos he's too clever and been doing it a long time." At that moment her phone beeped loudly. Amy looked startled. She picked up the phone and checked the text. "It's Dave just asking what time I start work. He always looks out for me, he's very protective of me; but I ain't got a boyfriend at the moment and he just makes sure when I'm in my flat that I'm alright. It's okay, I won't answer him just yet - I'll say I'm driving but I've got to phone him back soon or he'll get worried. So, Mick has all his joeys running around for him and they would never drop him in it. It's the guns that worry me and people getting really hurt because of them." "Right. So that's the guns and Mick. Anything about Dave, 'cos if he found out what you were telling us, he'd go mad." Amy went quiet. "I'm feeling really bad, but I have to tell you something," she said. "What is it?" queried Helen. "Dave is helping Mick," she admitted. "Like doing what?" Michelle pressed. "With things like telling him now and again about who the police are going to raid around the town." "Blimey," breathed Michelle. "How do you know that?" "'Cos I've been in Mick's house when he's been called by Dave and he's told me," Amy said. "That's bloody great!" exclaimed Helen. "Giving away our secrets." Amy could tell she was annoyed. "I know, and he's the one going to get into trouble too. I feel terrible telling you, but I had to tell someone." She began to cry. "This ain't easy doing this, you know," and she started sobbing. "I've gone against my two brothers, but it's just wrong and I hate it." Helen passed her a tissue box that was on a cabinet at the side of the room. "Well, there's plenty we can do to put a stop to it," said Michelle. "Why does Dave help him?" Amy had stopped crying and paused again.

"He's his brother to start with, and he also tells Dave what's going on in the town, so Dave gets good results. It makes Dave look good and keeps all the other dealers at bay so that Mick clears up. Mick also keeps him sweet with handouts, so the money helps Dave. He's only a PC so he's not on too much money." "Okay, I sort of get it," mused Michelle. "Like a brotherly love but with money and a bit of prestige for Dave 'cos it makes him look good at work, I'm getting it. Look Amy. It's one thing telling us stuff but another proving it, like turning this into evidence. Just so that we can start things rolling at our end, could you give us their mobile numbers, please? There's work we can do to help people investigate them. I promise you it won't come back on you. Trust me. So, you got their numbers, please?" Amy scrolled through her phone. "So, Mick's is 07869 497241 and...Dave's number is...07890 324517." "Thanks. And who knows those numbers?" Michelle asked. "Oh, loads of people, like the whole town has got those," said Amy. She had stopped crying by now. "It's just if we use them we need to know that it hasn't come from you," explained Helen. "Can you get anything else like registration numbers and addresses of their mates? It's all really useful for us." Amy nodded. "It shouldn't be a problem. Look, I'm going to have to go in a minute, I've got to get to work, I start at 1pm." "Where do you work?" asked Michelle. "At Evergreen Residential near the retail park. I'm a care assistant," Amy volunteered, adding, "I really love it, never thought I'd do that when I left school. The pay's crap but it's really worthwhile you know." "Yes," Michelle assured her. "That's what I'm going back to when I finish in this outfit. Lucky you." Amy got up from the chair she was sitting in, picked up her mobile phone from the table and checked the text. There weren't any new ones, but she knew she had to phone Dave back quickly. "Look. I've got to go 'cos of Dave. I'll phone you tomorrow if I get anything else." "Thanks so much for meeting us Amy, really appreciate your time and what you've told us. Phone me tomorrow and we can chat some more." Michelle gave Amy a piece of paper with her mobile number on it. "Put that in your phone under 'Gene Work' and then throw the bit of paper away." "Okay, no problem. I'm really sorry, I've gotta go!" and with that, Amy walked to the door, unlocked it and left the hotel room. She was in an obvious hurry, and had gone back into her nervous self again as she was when she first met them both.

"Blimey, what you make of that?" Michelle said to Helen. "Good stuff. Looks like Dave's in a bit of bother if we can prove any link between the two. Need to get some work done ASAP on the numbers and go from there." "I should say," agreed Michelle. "Let's get going and we can tell Martin the news on the way back in the car."

With that they gathered their bits, paid their dues and left the hotel. It had been a revealing meeting, the significance of which neither Michelle or Helen truly understood.

Chapter 15

Whilst Michelle and Helen were meeting their new informant, Josh and Andy were meeting Kayne. Josh had decided that it was going to be a quick meeting, just so Kayne could be paid the reward money he was owed for getting the details of the registration number he'd had checked the day before. Josh was getting more and more nervous and uncomfortable with all the corruption-related information that was floating around the office. Not only that, but Martin had decided Jim shouldn't know, and this was therefore an added worry for him. He was getting into territory he had never experienced before, so was further relying on his colleagues and Martin to ensure what he was doing was right. If the boss found out he was meeting Kayne and paying him money without him authorising it, as well as taking the type of information from him that he was, he would be finished in the team and possibly with his career too. It wasn't the most comfortable time he'd had in his service with Dorshire Police.

Josh had phoned Kayne that morning and arranged to meet him at 11am. This time Josh had told Kayne to go straight to the coffee shop just to save some time. This wasn't strictly what should happen, as every meeting with an informant should be carefully managed with the security of all parties involved as a top priority, but on this occasion Josh was in a rush. Josh and Andy had taken the reward money that they were going to pay Kayne from cashpoints using their covert company credit cards. There were strict protocols and policies in place, which both Josh and Andy could recite backwards, in order that they could not be accused of unlawfully taking money from the informant budget. It was just that on this occasion the boss hadn't authorised the payment of £400.

Josh and Andy got to the coffee shop at 10.55am to find Kayne already sitting at the table where they had last met him. They walked up to the table. Josh was nervous. Andy was as relaxed as ever; nothing ever flustered him.

Kayne stood up and greeted them with an "Alright lads, coffee's on me today!" he pronounced cheekily as he knew money was being paid to him. Josh and Andy smiled and sat down. They knew they wouldn't be allowing Kayne to buy anything for them, that was against the rules. "The usual, please," Kayne said to Andy as he went to buy the drinks. The mood was relaxed. Kayne knew he was going to get some money for doing his task and Josh knew that his informant had done well.

Andy returned to the table carrying three coffees. Kayne had already drunk one whilst he was waiting for them and his empty cup was on the table. It looked as though he had arrived at the venue particularly early. He only ever turned up early when he knew there was money to be given out and today he had been very early.

"So, you pleased with the stuff I gave you Josh?" he asked. "Good, wasn't it?" He was excited, and was one of those informants that wanted to please his handler. "Yes. Top drawer. Look, that's good stuff you got," Josh confirmed. "I haven't had any feedback yet but it's looking good. As long as you are safe and no one's going to find you out..." Josh suddenly realised what he had just done. He'd worked out that if the checks were carried out on the car belonging to the police, and someone was identified for doing the check, then someone somewhere would ask why a check was necessary on a covert police car, and why would anyone want such a check done? Josh suddenly wasn't as jovial. "Listen. What happened when you asked for the check to be done?" demanded Josh, urgently. "Well, the bloke didn't say a lot to be honest. He just asked how I got his number and how I knew Callum and that was it. Oh...and that if I wanted any more checks done, to get them done in the next couple of weeks as I wouldn't be able to get any more done soon, and that was it. It wasn't like difficult or anything, like he was very cool about it all, dead easy. So if you want me to do anything else just let me know. Straight forward money. So, have you got it?"

Kayne was cocky but at the same time nervous. He was also feeling a bit uncomfortable; this wasn't a normal situation for him. The realisation he'd just had, that he was involved with a corruption operation had spooked him somewhat. "I've got your money, Kayne, but just be careful. If you suddenly start splashing that amount around you might have to start explaining yourself," cautioned Josh. Kayne looked at Josh. He had regained a bit of composure and wanted to put on a brave front. "Listen. That ain't a lot, you worry too much. People nowadays where I come from and that I hang around with don't think anything of that sort of money. I started out doing this, like working for you two for the money, but now I just get a buzz out of doing it. Like none of my mates would ever think I'd be doing anything like this, not in a million years, not ever. I just like grassing up the really bad boys. You'll never get anything this good from anyone else. Ever! Love it." Josh was a bit taken aback. He thought he knew Kayne quite well, but it seemed that the relationship with him had moved on a bit since they first met in the cell when Josh had recruited him. Kayne was super-confident.

Informant and handler relationships always change over time. Josh had had the upper hand when they first met, but the dynamics had suddenly changed, and Josh hadn't experienced this before. Kayne was leading this conversation and Josh didn't feel in control. "Listen" Josh said. "I've got your money and we'd better cut it short today. I ain't put you through a route and it just doesn't feel right. I've got your money." Josh started counting out the money on the table when Andy chipped in. "Stop bloody counting out on the top and do it under the table next to him." Josh carried on and ignored Andy. "I'm nearly done mate. 280, 290, 300. 310, 320..." Andy got really annoyed. He knew Josh hadn't put Kayne through a route, had allowed him to get there early to the venue without challenging him about this and was then in broad daylight counting out £400 in view of the staff and other customers in the coffee shop. Not only had he just ignored his advice in front of the informant, but this was a nervous time for them all. Andy wasn't going to allow Josh to start taking short-cuts and then possibly get them all compromised by someone asking difficult questions about what they were doing, or even being spotted with Kayne. After all, this was the third time they'd met Kayne this week at the same time and in the same place and Andy had seen this type of complacency get colleagues in trouble before. He didn't want to have to do any more explaining if this bit went wrong too.

Josh came to the end of counting the money for Kayne, who agreed that it was £400 he'd just seen being put on the table. Kayne did the usual procedure, and signed a receipt that Josh passed him in his pseudonym 'Billy Bonds'. He then put his left thumb on a small inkpad that Josh gave him and put his thumbprint in a small box which was in the bottom left of the receipt and that was that. The formalities of Josh paying Kayne were done. Kayne folded the wad of money in half and put it in his wallet.

"Thanks" he said to Josh. "If there's anything else you want me to do that's as easy as that, just let me know! That was the easiest 400 quid I've ever earnt," he crowed. Josh smiled. "Yeh. Not bad, is it? It's just that I don't want you getting found out for getting this check done." What he hadn't told Kayne was, that he'd asked him to get a covert police car number checked, and if it was ever found that it was Kayne that had asked for the check, he would have to come up with a better story apart from him wanting to have a check done.

Kayne stood up. This was mirrored by Josh and Andy who were sitting at the opposite side of the table to Kayne. "Right lads. Looks like it's a short one today. If I get anything else, I'll give you a bell. I'm free tomorrow if you want to meet up." Kayne shook their hands and walked out of the coffee shop.

As soon as Kayne was out of the shop Andy started on Josh. "Listen. You've got a great source in Kayne who is giving us some top rate information, but you just lost control there. He's turned up early, picked where we were sitting, led the conversation, I could go on. This isn't the easiest of times for you and me and the rest of the office, but one thing I will let you know is this. I'm not going to let standards slip just because you can't be bothered to do things properly. You'll get us in even *more* trouble if it all goes wrong. I think we might be in a lot anyway if Jim gets wind of what's going on - he'll go absolutely mad. But I don't want him even *more* maddened if he found out we weren't doing what we were meant to be doing and then doing it badly!" Josh laughed. "I get it and I'm sorry. It's just that I don't think I'm coping well with this sort of pressure. I just want to meet Kayne, do what we have to do and get out of it. I'm not liking things right now; it's all a bit spooky." Andy looked at Josh. "Really? You surprise me," he said with sarcasm in his voice. "Look, I've seen it all before. When you get juicy corruption bits like this, the powers that be will catch the corrupt ones. That's what makes this the best job in the force - stick with it. Just ask me for any help you need, but whatever you do, don't take any short-cuts because believe you me, we'll come unstuck and get caught out somewhere down the line." Josh looked at Andy knowingly. "Yep, you're right. I don't know if we will meet him again next week, but next time I'll definitely be doing it properly."

The two left the coffee shop and got into their car. Little did they know that whilst they had been meeting and paying Kayne for what he had provided earlier in the week, Michelle and Helen had gathered some revealing information which had taken the investigation a lot further and might have just made the link between what was happening in Kayne's part of Padmouth and the part of Padmouth that was the domain of PC Dave Harrison.

Chapter 16

It was late morning and Jim was working from home. This was a perk some officers of a supervisory rank in Dorshire Police used on an increasingly common basis to get away from the stresses of being in the office. Jim was no different, and not being in a uniformed role meant this was easier for him to do than others.

He was sitting at home at the dining-room table and had been up early, typing his report in preparation for the Surveillance Commissioner coming to inspect his team the following week. He'd had a late evening the night before and was tired. Jim had also been through a stressful few weeks and hadn't slept well. There was far more to learn in his new role than he had realised beforehand and it had been a steep learning curve. It wasn't just a case of him reading the intelligence the informants provided including the decision-making that came with it, but the safety of each informant plus the safety of the informant handlers he had to manage. He had also underestimated the tremendous pressure the team was under to produce relevant intelligence the directorate could use to tackle the ever-changing force requirements.

Jim's teenage children had left early and had both gone to school. Lorraine was out shopping and had left him in peace to get on with his work. He wished that she could have busied herself for the day so he could just get on with what he had to do. If she was in the house she would just fuss and get on his nerves. He loved her dearly but she irritated him with her mumsy ways.

He had got quite a bit done but he put himself under a lot of pressure to make sure the inspection went well. He didn't want to have a bad report, especially as it was his first. This inspection could be the difference between him attaining the next rank or not. He had only been in the role for a few weeks and the results the team had had he knew would all be credited to them and the work of his predecessor Dan; but he would ensure that he would put his name to it all.

He was getting hungry and his stomach felt like his 'throat had been cut'. He'd had a small waffle for breakfast, but it hadn't touched the sides. As he sat at the table he kicked one of the cats out from under his feet as it had been very annoying. He knew it wouldn't be returning to bother him.

It was now 11.38am. Jim had been typing away, deep in thought, when heard a car pull up on the drive. He looked up from his laptop and could just see the top half of Lorraine's powder blue car; she was home. His heart sank. He heard the driver's door close and saw Lorraine walk round to the back of the car to get the shopping out. He could feel himself becoming irritated at seeing her, not because of her, but he knew he would now be interrupted for the rest of the day with her busying herself around the house.

The boot of the car slammed shut and a short while later he heard the key turn in the front door. The door opened and he heard the rustle of carrier bags as Lorraine came into the house. She put them down in the hallway and closed the door behind her. The door slammed shut with some force as it was caught in the wind. The whole house seemed to reverberate with the force of the door slamming against the frame.

Lorraine was her happy, normal self as she came home. "Hi, love," she said quite loudly as she took the bags of shopping from the hallway into the kitchen. "Everything okay?" Jim pretended he hadn't heard her. "You okay, love?" she called again. "Yep!" came his sharp reply. His Scottish accent accentuated his gruffness. She knew he wasn't in a chatty frame of mind as he was buried in his work. She thought it best to leave him to it and started emptying the bags, hearing the keyboard clicking from the dining room as she unpacked the shopping. Lorraine hated any atmosphere in the house. Jim was not the chattiest of husbands at the best of times, but she had noticed over the last few weeks he had been particularly grumpy. They hadn't really been getting on since she picked him up from the pub at Dan's leaving do last Friday.

A few minutes went by and she finished the unpacking. The carrier bags were kept in a cupboard under the stairs in the hallway and she went to put them away. As she did so she glanced up and saw Jim continuing to type on his laptop. He was deep in thought, but she decided a cup of tea might cheer him up. Maybe he hadn't had time to make one all morning whilst she had been out. It was nearly lunchtime and perhaps she would make him a cuppa and then prepare some lunch so he could have a break and they could have a spot of time catching up. She popped her head around the door from the kitchen into the dining-room. "Cuppa tea, love?" she asked. There was a pause. "Yep. Thanks," he said.

Lorraine went back into the kitchen and put the kettle on. At least it gave her something to do whilst he carried on typing. This was a day she had taken off work so that they could do something nice together, but work came first, and he was the one who wanted promotion. Once he had reached the next rank they would be financially better off and maybe this would put his promotion aspirations on hold for a couple of years. They could then spend some quality time as a couple and as a family too. The girls hadn't seen a lot of him as he had progressed through the ranks and as a result were somewhat distant from him. Lorraine knew Jim had a reputation for being a disciplinarian at work and he brought home some of the same attitude towards his daughters. This had extended over time towards her as well, and although she resented him for it, she knew this was the price she had to pay to keep the family as a unit and the girls with a mother and father that hadn't separated. This was common in the police where both worked for the force and the stresses and strains of shift work and the work itself took its' toll on couples.

Lorraine had prepared two mugs with a tea bag in each. Jim took his tea with one sugar, nothing more, nothing less. The kettle was the type they boiled on their gas hob and Jim wanted it made so he would know it hadn't been brewed. He didn't like his milk being put in the mug before the tea had a chance to brew either, and he knew if she did this it wouldn't taste the same.

By now the kettle was boiling. It was rather old-fashioned in a way, and the moment the whistle blew and made a screech, Lorraine turned it off.

She poured the boiling water into the mug – it had 'World's Best Dad' written on the side as Jim had been given it as a Father's Day present from the girls. She knew Jim hadn't had any breakfast, so she thought he just might like some of his favourite biscuits. She went to the cupboard and placed a packet on a side plate. She finished making the tea and took both mugs into the dining room. As she approached Jim at the table she could see that he remained engrossed in his work. He didn't look up. She became nervous as she walked towards him as she knew he wasn't in the best of moods. Her hands trembled slightly as she went towards the table and bent down to put his mug and biscuits next to him. As she did so, she spilt a small amount of tea on one of the reports that was to the right-hand side of the laptop.

Jim stopped typing. He sat still and stared straight ahead. He slowly reached towards Lorraine and then grabbed her left hand. She stood still, frozen to the spot. The blood drained from her face. She was petrified.

Jim was raging, and she feared what he would do next.

Jim wrapped his right hand around her left hand and started to squeeze it tightly. He gradually increased the pressure until the bones started to crack with the force that he was exerting. The tears started to well in her eyes with the pain.

"Don't you ever, *ever* do that again," he said. "I'm trying to fucking work and you have interrupted my bloody day. Get out of my sight." He released his grip. Lorraine's left hand was white where the blood had drained from it. She found it hard to uncurl her fingers due to the pain. The tears rolled down her cheeks and dripped off her chin. She couldn't talk.

Lorraine turned and walked back into the kitchen. She felt like she had a knot in her stomach and felt sick; her head was spinning and she didn't know what to do. Maybe it was best for her to just get out of the house and go for a drive she thought; just go anywhere to get away from Jim. Get away from the man who she called her husband but who had turned into someone who continually, and on a steadily more frequent basis hurt her. *Just get away*, she thought. She grabbed the car keys she had placed on the worktop in the kitchen after she had come in from shopping, picked up her handbag and headed for the front door, taking her coat with her as she hurriedly walked through the hallway. There was no way she would be going back in the house whilst Jim was there. She had had enough and would stay with her sister for the night, she thought. The girls were old enough now and would have to look after themselves. Jim wouldn't be of any help.

Lorraine opened the front door and looked behind her. She could see Jim through the glass panels in the dining room door. He sipped his tea and carried on typing. What he had just done to her had caused her to lose the small amount of love she had left for him. This was the final straw, and regardless of his career or keeping the family together as a unit, she there and then decided she would face life without him; she closed the front door and got into her car. As she drove away from the house she felt a strange sense of relief. Never would she have to put up with being treated like that again; the next move would be for her to report it to the police.

Jim carried on typing his report, drank his tea and had a few of the biscuits she had brought him. He heard the front door close and the car drive away. Lorraine must have popped out to see her sister and then to collect the girls from school he thought. Jim was still hungry but decided he could hang on for a few hours - he liked her cooking and she would be back in a couple of hours to make the dinner.

Chapter 17

Keith was sitting in his office. He was having an indifferent sort of day; not bad but not good. There had been no answers yet to anything Martin had come to see him about earlier and he was waiting for Rob to update him. Maybe there was nothing in it and it was just several coincidental happenings that had all come together in some sort of strange alignment. It had been three hours since he had asked him to carry out a check and Rob was taking longer than normal to get back to him. He was becoming slightly impatient and decided to phone Rob. "Rob. It's Keith. How are you getting on with that check?" There was a bit of a silence. "Rob?" "Yes, boss, sorry; and sorry for the delay in getting back to you. It's just that I'm checking and triple checking my facts." "Well, what've you got?" said Keith. "I've done a check on who last looked at that registration and it goes down to a civilian who works in The Traffic Process Unit," explained Rob. "Blimey," said Keith. "Any more?" "Yes, boss. She checked it mid-afternoon yesterday. She only looked at the front page on the screen like who it goes down to and their address. It's a VW Golf that goes down to a local company." "And what's her name?" "Marie Solomon. I've done some background on her and she has worked for Dorshire Police for eight years. There's nothing on her. No disciplinary investigations, nothing. I've got her personal details up on the screen now. She's single and lives in

131

Padmouth. I've got a landline and mobile number for her if you want them?" "Yes, please." Keith scribbled down the two numbers that Rob read out. "That's it for the minute. Many thanks." Keith put the phone down; he took a deep breath and sat looking at the numbers. This job would be going somewhere, and for starters Marie Solomon would be getting in trouble; but there may be more than just this check. Padmouth seemed to be coming to the fore in its' fair share of involvement with this corruption job, and maybe Martin's hunch that the two jobs might be connected may have some merit after all.

Keith picked up the phone again. He needed to speak to Martin and needed to do it quickly; he dialled his number. Martin was at his desk in the office with only him and Ellie sitting there. Everyone else was out and Jim hadn't yet come into the office. They were busying themselves with their work when Martin's phone rang, breaking the silence. Martin could see on his screen who was dialling him and he picked up the phone. "Hello, boss. What can I do for you?" "Martin. I've got something that needs sorting and it might just tie in with the other stream of reporting that you have there. Can you pop over to the office and I'll talk it through with you". "What, now?" asked Martin. "Yes please. It's pretty urgent." "I'll be right over," said Martin. He put the phone down and gathered his paperwork together. "Ellie. I'm just popping out for a bit to the Anti-Corruption Unit's office. If anyone asks, I've just gone to see the finance department. I won't be long." "Alright. Everything okay?" she asked. "Hope so," he answered, and left the office.

Martin walked quickly across the car park to Keith's office. He could tell by the tone of Keith's voice he had something worthwhile to talk about; he knew his hunch about the two informants being linked somehow was possibly correct and they were starting to get to the bottom of what was going on.

He walked into the Anti-Corruption Unit's building and went to Keith's office. He knocked on the door and waited a short time before being called in. Martin entered, closed the door behind him and sat down in front of Keith in that now familiar comfy chair. "So, I've got the results back from the checks that Rob's done and it's looking quite good, or bad depending on which way you look at it. The check that was done on your covert VW was made by a civilian in the Traffic Process Unit; her name is Marie Solomon. We've done a bit of digging and she lives in Padmouth. She's the daughter of Pete Solomon; he used to be in the force but left due to a bad back. Don't know if you remember him?" "No, boss. Don't think I do," said Martin. "Well, we had a few bits on him over the years, but nothing that ever went anywhere," said Keith. "I've got a feeling that we could be onto something more serious than just Marie doing a check on your VW."

Just then Martin's mobile phone rang. "Do you mind if I take this, boss, please? It's Michelle and hopefully she is updating me with the outcome of her meeting with 'Susan'." Keith nodded. "Hello, you okay?" Martin asked Michelle. She sounded excited and started relaying the details of the meeting she and Helen had just finished. "Hold on," Martin said . "I'm with DCI Keith Catlin in his office, I'll just put you on speaker phone." Martin pushed the speaker button his device and placed the phone on Keith's desk. "Go on, you're on speaker phone now; we're listening."

Michelle was in the car with Helen on the way back to the office. "Well, it's like this, boss. We've just finished meeting our new informant and she said her name is Susan but her real name is Amy; she's the sister of PC Dave Harrison and Mick Harrison. She's told us about some guns Mick has in his possession and that Dave tips him off about any raids that are going to happen in Padmouth; it's all stuff that can be researched. She's given us mobile numbers for both Mick and Dave and is quite happy for us to get back to her again and ask for anything else that might help us out." Martin looked at Keith and smiled. "And what's the reason she wants to help us out?" he asked. "She's just fed up with the stuff they are doing and knows it's wrong, and now that Mick has got guns and has started firing them in the woods where he lives, she thinks someone is going to get seriously hurt soon. She's upset about what they are doing and wants to help. It's not easy for her doing this but she seems like a nice girl. Well, I say girl, but she's in her mid-twenties. Sorry, I forgot to ask exactly how old she is, I'll ask when I speak to her again." "Great, cheers," said Martin. "That's excellent information; you've both done very well getting it. How long will it be before you are back at the office?" "We are only 10 minutes away," said Michelle. "Okay, I'll see you both when you get back. Can you come straight to DCI Keith Catlin's office please." Martin picked up his phone and checked to make sure the conversation had finished.

"What do you think of that?" he said to Keith. "Mmm - looks like we have a job on here. When they give us the mobile numbers I'll get Rob to do some checks on the numbers for Mick and Dave and see if there are any links between them and Marie Solomon. It'll be interesting to see if there are and when the calls were made; also if there are any other links from them to anyone else."

Martin looked thoughtful. He knew Paul Slacke was Marie Solomon's supervisor within the Traffic Process Unit, but it would be a big leap of faith to even suggest that he was in some way linked to her committing an illegal check on a vehicle. "You know boss, Marie's supervisor is Paul Slacke. He is an experienced Sergeant, and this is the sort of thing he would know she would be doing. I think they do random tests of who is doing what checks and for what reason, so he'd pick up on this sort of thing." Martin was aware of what Paul Slacke was like, that he wasn't the hardest worker the force had ever employed, so it wouldn't be unreasonable to think he wouldn't have checked Marie's work. "If you want my thoughts about where this is going, I'll give you them, if that's alright?" Even though Keith was a DCI and Martin was a Sergeant, he was open to debate and discussion. He didn't have all the answers to all the issues he had to deal with and was happy for Martin to offer his opinion. "Yes. I'm all ears." Martin continued; "If Rob finds that there's a link between either Mick or Dave Harrison and Marie, then I think they should be arrested straight away for Misconduct in a Public Office. This will stop them causing any more problems immediately, and then we can see what drops out of that. We can get their phones, find out what's on them and see what they say. It all seems pretty straightforward now; it looks like Mick has checks done for him by Dave, who somehow gets them done by Marie. I don't know what the link could be between Marie and the two brothers, but that may come out of any further investigation." Keith looked at Martin. "You're probably not far off what I was thinking. I'll get things arranged for some executive action as and when we need it and get it sorted in case we need it for this afternoon. I'll get Rob to come up to the office and he can be here when your two get back." He picked up the phone and called Rob. "Rob. It's Keith. Can you get up here now, please? Things are moving on a bit quick and it needs your expert help."

Just then there was a knock at the door. "Come in," said Keith; it was Michelle and Helen at the door. As they walked in, Rob was close behind them. "Come in everyone." They all came into Keith's office and stood around the chair where Martin was sitting. "Right, gang. We've got some interesting developments with some information that Michelle and Helen have gathered this morning. Rob has done some great work researching other information that Martin's team has provided this week, and it looks increasingly like the two streams of reporting are linked. If Michelle and Helen can brief Rob here, I'll get things moving to ensure we can sort things out this afternoon. Great work, guys. Just make sure we keep it all very tight and not tell anyone what's going on. Everyone happy?" They all nodded. Keith got up and walked out of his office.

Martin looked at everyone. "All okay?" "Yes, Sarge," said Michelle. "Good. Right, Michelle. If you could brief Rob about what you were told earlier, he can then get on and do some checks. I'll make sure that if anything is going to happen then I'll keep you all informed." Michelle began telling Rob the details that she had been given that morning whilst Rob made notes; when she had finished Rob left and went back to his office.

Martin looked at Michelle and Helen. "Great work. This job looks like it's going places. If Marie is safe and no harm comes to her, then happy days. Shall we go back to the office for a coffee?" Helen looked pleased. "Oh yes, just what I need - and some lunch too, I'm starving!" Michelle laughed. "You're not the only one!" They all left Keith's office and walked back to theirs. It had been an eventful morning and things were moving on at a pace.

Chapter 18

Josh and Andy had already returned to the office by the time Martin, Michelle and Helen arrived. They had settled back at their desks and were making small talk as the rest of the team walked in. "Hi, guys," said Martin to the lads. "Yep, all good," said Josh. "Well, sort of," added Andy. "What's up?" Martin enquired. Andy was just about to start telling him of his concerns about Kayne and how things were developing with him, when Josh cut across Andy. "Oi! If you are going to say what I think you are going to say you can stop there. Sarge, I think that we are all getting a bit edgy with what's going on and we just must keep it real. Like I don't mind saying in front of everyone, I just feel a bit uncomfortable keeping all this from the boss and doing stuff behind his back. I mean if he found out, then we would..." Martin chipped in. "Guys. I get it. Things have really moved on in the last couple of days, and even today we've got some stuff that is really concerning. The thing about the boss not knowing I completely get, but you must just trust me. I've dealt with corruption jobs before and it's just the way it is; if nothing comes of it, then so be it. If it does, then I'll deal with it myself. You'll all have my backing, and I'll tell anyone who asks that you were acting on my instructions. The boss will have to deal with me as he sees fit, but I also have cover from Keith Catlin in the Anti-Corruption Unit. The boss will probably be back tomorrow morning, but by then there may have been some action against some of those who've been possibly implicated in whatever they may have or not done. In the meantime, just type up your contact records away from his prying eyes and I'll manage them."

Martin hadn't even got to his desk to sit down when his phone rang. He walked quickly to his desk and picked up his phone. "Hello." It was Keith. "Martin; things are moving on really quickly. Just to put you in the picture, Rob has done some research on those numbers that Michelle gave to Rob and he has come up with some interesting links. Dave's mobile number phoned an unidentified mobile number yesterday afternoon just before the check was done on the VW. I'm thinking that Dave has phoned Marie and got her to make the check. So it's looking like Dave is going to get arrested this afternoon along with Marie. We can't afford for them to potentially do any more harm, so I've made the decision to have them both nicked; we'll see what happens after that. We've got monitoring put on all three of their numbers, so after they're arrested we will see what follows. I'll keep you updated. They'll both get nicked at work. Should be interesting!" Keith was very matter of fact and had been involved before with the arrest of staff whilst they were at work. He was keen to do this, as it sent out a strong message to others, and on this occasion was confident they had a decent job that couldn't be refuted. "Sure, boss; just let me know what happens and I'll pass it on to the team."

Martin put the phone down; he looked pleased. At last Dorshire Police were doing something about the corruption he had suspected had been going on for some time, and it was the CO15 team that on this occasion was leading the way. The team could see the pleasure on his face. "You okay Sarge?" said Helen. "Yep, thanks. All good. Looks like they are going to finally do something about the bent idiots in this job that don't do us all any favours. I'll let you know how they get on." The team were nervous. This was a time when their informants were most vulnerable, when executive action resulted from their information. This was when the finger pointing all started; however, this was why they were in the role, for these moments when all the risk and hard work was worth it, and particularly on this occasion when it was helping to root out corrupt members of staff.

Martin sat down in his seat. He could feel a sense of satisfaction that they had at least reached this point. What would be would be, and hopefully any investigation would get to the bottom of anyone committing wrongdoing.

Chapter 19

Paul Slacke looked at his watch; it was 3.18pm. He had already stayed too long in the office for his liking, and normally would have gone home by this time, but even by his own standards knew he'd had an extended lunch break and didn't want to get into trouble with any boss. He knew Martin had seen him in the canteen, and anything he could do to bad-mouth him or give him any ammunition to discredit him he thought, Martin might just do that.

He started tidying his desk and shuffling items around. He looked up and could see his small team of administrative clerks typing away at their desks. One of them was Marie Solomon. She was a conscientious worker who Paul had known for a long time as her dad Pete had worked with Paul when they were on the Padmouth Taskforce and had kept in touch. Marie was a quiet and shy person who just got on with her job. She was young and naïve, and kept herself to herself; this job suited her just fine. She had experienced a few mental health issues after leaving school a couple years before, and Paul had done Pete a favour by giving her a job. She had only been there for a few months and there hadn't been any dramas with her – she was just a steady person who did as she was told and gave her boss Paul no issues.

Just then the door of the office opened. There stood a uniformed Sergeant and three of his team. They walked in purposefully towards Paul Slacke's desk. The Sergeant spoke to Paul. I'm looking for Marie Solomon." Paul looked shocked. He pointed her out in front of her desk. "Marie. These guys have asked to speak to you." The colour in Marie's face suddenly disappeared and she sank in her chair; she seemed genuinely shocked to see the uniformed Sergeant in the office. He walked up to her with one of his team. The female officer was nervous too. She said, "Marie Solomon. I'm arresting you on suspicion of Misconduct in a Public Office. You do not have to say anything, but it may harm your defence if you do not mention when questioned something you later rely on in court. Anything you do say may be given in evidence." Marie started crying. "But I haven't done anything," she said. "What's this all about? I just can't believe this. Paul. What's this all about?"

Paul sat in his chair. He was staring straight ahead of him and straight through Marie; he was silent. Marie looked at him. "What's going on, Paul? You'd better get me out of this." Marie stood up; she was crying. The female officer asked her to leave her desk and walk with her out of the office. The rest of the office were in shock; none of them could believe what was going on and what they were witnessing. Marie was the newest and youngest member of their team and not the sort they would ever suspect of doing anything wrong, let alone be arrested - and now, here she was being led away by a uniformed officer. Never had this happened in this office and they had no idea what was going on.

The officer escorted Marie out of the office. The Sergeant spoke to Paul. "Can we have a word outside, please?" "Of course," Paul said nervously in his Irish accent; he was visibly shaking. He knew the Sergeant from old but hadn't seen him for a few years and had forgotten his name. The two walked out of the office and stood in the car park adjoining the building. "I don't know what this is about, but if there's anything you know that could help her out now's the time to sort things out for her." Paul said. "She is a great girl; doesn't need anything like this. I used to work with her dad Pete Solomon on the Padmouth Task Force. Top man, a great guy. If you could just get hold of custody before she gets there and if things could be sorted out, I'm sure all involved would be grateful." "Aye. I'll see what I can do" agreed the Sergeant.

The two parted and Paul went back into the office. His team weren't doing any work and were chatting nervously to each other. "Guys. Just to say I don't know what's going on, but obviously we are all shocked by what's happened. I'll try and find out and let you all know in the morning. If you all want to go home, I'll clear away and lock up."

The team all hurriedly cleared their desks and went home; this workday was the strangest they had ever had. There were a few in tears as they left the building.

Paul remained in the office. He slumped in his chair and looked straight ahead. He had a vacant, empty look; he was drained. He reached into his bottom drawer and took out a bottle of whisky that only had a quarter left in it. He placed it on his desk and unscrewed the cap. He picked up the bottle and took a swig. He took another. He picked up his mobile phone, scrolled through his address book and started to write a text message. "Boss. Just had the HQ Arrest Team in my office. They've nicked Marie Solomon for Misconduct. Don't know what's going to happen. Nothing I can do. Will let you know when I know what's happening next." Paul sent the text and waited. A minute later, he received a reply. "Oh. You're clean aren't you?" Paul replied, "Yes. Unless she says anything. No trace." The reply came back with a smiley face emoji. Paul felt a little better. He knew Marie wouldn't say anything and that she would take it. He was as safe as houses and the job couldn't touch him. He had many friends in high places and it would be his word against hers in terms of her saying that he'd asked her to do a check the previous afternoon. She wouldn't have a leg to stand on. She was a vulnerable character who wouldn't have the bottle to say anything against him and even if she did, who would believe her? Paul took another swig from the bottle. He could feel the warm whisky trickling down the inside of his throat and into his stomach. He'd been shocked to see his uniformed colleagues in his office taking away a member of his team, but when he had thought about it a bit more and he'd had a few more swigs of whisky from his bottle, he felt a lot better.

At the same time as uniformed officers walked into Paul Slacke's office, PC Dave Harrison was tidying his desk in the multi-agency building in Padmouth. He'd just had another day at the office, having been part of the multi-agency Padmouth Task-Force for just over six years and knew the job as well as any of his colleagues, and knew it inside out. He was virtually part of the furniture. His desk was near the door in prime position in the office so he could see everything that was going on in front of him. He assumed the physical position where the supervisor should sit, but the rest of the team had their desks further back in the room. Harrison was unpopular in the office but as he had been working there for such a long time, his colleagues tolerated him. He was the only police officer left as the financial cuts had taken their toll here too. A few years before, a team of six officers led by Jim Fowler were gradually reduced in number as the budget cuts had started to bite. Harrison was a tall, strapping officer who had high standards, with buffed shiny shoes and creases on his shirt that could have sliced through butter like a knife. He had a presence in the office he'd used to great effect in getting to know his female co-workers. He got to know each one as a steady stream of them had started, and then left the team; this was a pattern which had gone on for several years.

Harrison was sitting at his desk, preparing to leave a bit early – just as he normally did. Out the corner of his eye through the office window, he noticed a white marked Dorshire Police van pull up in the car park. He thought this slightly unusual, as they weren't due to come to the office that afternoon. In fact, they hardly ever visited the office.

He stood up from his desk and walked towards the door to greet his colleagues, some of whom he recognised as they had worked in Padmouth over the last few years. He waited in the corporate entrance to the office and watched them through the glass doors. He saw the team get out of the van and walk towards the building and towards him. They all had stern expressions on their faces, not the normal, happy, jovial faces that they generally had when they came to the coastal town.

One of them approached Harrison. "PC Dave Harrison. I am arresting you on suspicion of Misconduct in a Public Office. You do not have to say anything, but it may harm your defence if you do not mention when questioned something you later rely on in court."

Harrison collapsed to the floor. His legs gave way at these words and he fell where he was standing. The team of four officers quickly put him in the recovery position. Harrison had fainted but soon came round. One of the officers went down a corridor leading off the main entrance hall and returned with an office chair to where the incident was taking place. One of the arrest team lifted him onto the chair as he continued to improve. "Listen, guys, and thank you. I know what you've had to do and you're only doing your job; I'm not going to make a scene. Just get me in the van and get me out of here, please. I just need my keys and that's it. Just get me out of here." Tears started to run down his face; he was a broken man. This was in stark contrast to his stature and his smart police uniform.

By this time, the other workers in the office had huddled around the water dispenser which was in the corner of the office near the fire door. They were all looking over to what was happening by the main door of the building just beyond the other side of the room. Although they were interested none seemed to be overly concerned, as he was seen as a workshy bully in the office who had gotten away with a lot for far too long. Harrison had been a ladies' man, but any relationship he'd had didn't last as they had all seen through him very quickly. Although the staff hadn't heard what had happened and what he had been arrested for, there was not a lot of love lost between those in the office and Harrison.

The small team of officers sent to arrest Harrison searched his desk. They seized various items of paperwork together with his mobile phone. Harrison pointed out where his bunch of keys were in the bottom drawer before the officers took them too. He was looking around the office at his colleagues as he awaited his own removal.

He could see them staring at him.

"Listen, guys. I'm really sorry for what's happened and having to put you through this. I'm going to see you all again very soon hopefully and explain what's gone on. There is an explanation for all of this and I hope you'll understand what has led to this mess. I'm so sorry." No one replied to him. There was complete silence from them all.

The arrest team led Harrison away, out of the room and out of the building, his head bowed and feet barely lifting off the floor as he shuffled towards the van. The team placed him inside via the back doors, which slammed shut behind him. The officers got in and all the doors slammed shut with the familiar tinny sound that police van doors make.

The office workers slowly returned to their desks. The significance of Harrison's empty desk where he had been sitting could not be underestimated; it felt like a weight lifted from the office. He had been a somewhat unsavoury presence in the team, and more so as he had no police supervisor; hence he thought he was in charge. The team chatted. The consensus was that it would be better if Harrison didn't come back at any time and try to explain his behaviour. There could be no excuses for his antics over the years and as a police officer he should have behaved accordingly. The Padmouth Taskforce had once been a beacon of excellence, but it's reputation had become tarnished in recent years; this was just the final nail in the coffin. The police van slowly pulled away from the car park and disappeared out of sight. The windows were blackened so anyone inside could not be seen. No-one could see Harrison inside. On the side the words 'Proud to Serve' were printed.

Those who saw the van transporting Harrison were unaware of what it represented. The journey was a long one for Harrison. Force policy was that any officer arrested had to be taken to a police station on the furthest side of the county from where they were based. This minimised any possible contact with those the arrested officer may know and lessened any embarrassment, both for the officer and the force. It didn't always work out according to plan, but at least it was a help. However, Harrison was well known; he knew many people, and it wouldn't take long for word to spread across the force that he had been arrested. It wouldn't take long inside the force, or outside it for that matter.

Harrison knew the journey to custody would take just over an hour to complete. He would have plenty of thinking time to contemplate what had just happened. Not only that, but he would have a good deal of time after arriving to prepare what he was going to say in interview. Every copper dreaded such a moment. For his whole career he had been doing the arresting, and now the tables were turned. The humility, the degradation, the fall from grace, and the realisation that his career was at an end were all too real. He knew his life would never be the same again. What would his friends and family think? What would prison be like? The answers just spun in his head; he wasn't in a good place.

The van seemed to hit every bump in the road. Harrison sat on a wooden bench, with the jolting caused by the road surface jarring through his spine. He was sweating with nerves; he felt sick and his throat was parched. He kept clenching his fists as if he was angry, but this was just an involuntary reaction to the situation. He just stared at the floor. The journey seemed to take forever. He didn't speak to anyone during the journey; he was the only prisoner in the van. He looked at his watch; it was 4.32pm. Harrison knew he would be arriving at the custody area of Midway Police Station soon. He knew what the procedure would be, and he wasn't expecting to be welcomed with open arms.

It didn't take long before he heard the engine slowing and becoming quieter. The van came to a stop, as it waited for the blue security gates to the backyard area of the police station to slowly open. Security was always particularly tight at this station as it was the high- security station for the force. It was the one designated to interview terrorist suspects and anyone of any great note. Not that Harrison had yet been elevated to that status, but nonetheless having higher than usual security meant he shouldn't be subject to unnecessary interference from supervisors who would just be checking to make sure that he was "alright". They wouldn't have the access to the custody area as their electronic access passes would be denied. Harrison had heard this had been the case with officers arrested for corruption offences, and that they'd had friendly visits as a reminder to keep their mouths shut. Harrison wasn't in the frame of mind to be having visits from anyone, let alone supervisory officers. He hoped the press wouldn't find out he was in there and be waiting for him when he was released.

The van pulled into the back yard of the police station and reversed slowly so that the back doors would open directly into the custody-holding bay. Harrison heard the reversing sensor alarm making a shrill noise. It cut through him and resonated through his body. The van stopped and the back doors opened. What was left of the daylight, managed to creep into the back of the van. His whole body felt stiff as he slowly got up from the bench and took a couple of paces towards the metal tread that he used to step down onto the concrete floor. The cold air hit him as he exited the van. He shuffled a few yards towards the back of the holding bay. The officers led him through a set of blue vertical metal gates and into the oh-so-familiar surroundings of the bleak custody area. The smell of the place was also familiar to Harrison - a mixture of dried blood and cleaning fluid, an unpleasant smell. The rubberised floor was an off-yellow colour and the walls were turquoise blue. In front of him, he could see a custody desk. He paused for a minute and stood next to the arresting officer who was escorting him. He could see at the end of the long corridor the back of a female prisoner that had just been booked in. Her long hair falling down her back shook, and he could hear her uncontrollable sobbing while being led away to a cell. Harrison didn't know it but this was Marie Solomon. He had never met, spoken to her or even knew of her, but even so he felt her anguish.

The last few steps towards the custody desk would be the longest he had ever taken. He gulped, but there was nothing to swallow. He looked at the Custody Sergeant as she stared at him from an elevated position behind her desk. At least he didn't recognise her he thought. "What's your name, please?" she asked. The rest of the conversation was just a blur to Harrison as she went through the booking-in procedure he knew only too well. He just kept thinking and wondering how his life had come to this. How did he end up standing there, knowing he was shortly going to have to explain to his colleagues what possessed him to do what he had done? What could he possibly say by way of reasonable explanation? Harrison knew it all, he knew exactly what the course of events had been that had led him to this point. But this was not the time for him to start trying to get others out of the mire. This was a very real situation that he now found himself in. He was facing the probability of losing his job as well as a possible prison sentence. The sound of the Custody Sergeant's voice seemed as if it was in the distance, as if someone was talking to him from afar. Harrison was too busy considering his immediate future and what he was going to say in interview. He was already thinking ahead. He thought perhaps he wouldn't be interviewed that evening, but would still have plenty time to think about things. "Would you like anyone informed that you are here?" the Custody Sergeant enquired. Harrison paused. He was single and there was no one at home. Who *did* he want to know? He thought long and hard; there was no rush. He smiled knowingly and was about to say a name but he stopped. He looked at the Custody Sergeant. "Can I have a think about that, please? I might just do that later on." "Of course," she answered. "That's not a problem, just ask, and as long as it's all right and not going to interfere with why you are here and the investigation, then we can do it anytime." "Okay," he said. "I'll have a think and get back to you. Thanks."

Harrison turned around and one of the gaolers led him to Cell 7. As he walked along the corridor to his cell, he could hear the sound of uncontrollable crying from the cell opposite. It sounded dreadful. He assumed it was the woman booked in before him; custody was a strange environment for anyone. Maybe this was the first time she'd been nicked, it was the same for him too, he thought.

He went into the cell and heard the clunk of the huge metal blue door close behind him. He didn't feel fearful any more.

He knew what he had to do to help himself. This was his time.

Chapter 20

Paul Slacke had remained in his office long after the arrest of Marie Solomon and the rest of his team had gone home. He looked at the clock on the far wall in the office; it was 5.40pm. Paul sat at his computer looking through random e-mails and briefings, none of which was of any great interest to him. He was waiting to see if he could find any information on Marie, and when she had been booked into custody. Paul was able to see the computer records, and if she had made any comments when she had been booked in. He also knew the records would show if there were any welfare concerns about her. He wasn't strictly allowed to do this, but thought if anyone asked him why he was doing it, he would say he was checking her record as her supervisor to see if there was anything he could do to support her.

Paul kept nervously refreshing the screen. All of a sudden at 5.44pm, the record appeared at the bottom of the list of those that were in custody at Midway Police Station. There were seven prisoners in custody and the screen showed for what offence. He clicked on her specific record to reveal more details. He could see when and where she had been arrested, for what offence, and the name of the arresting officer. He could also see her arrest was for Misconduct in a Public Office. Knowing this could attract a custodial sentence if she were convicted as it was a serious matter, he scrolled down to the comments section. This was a specific section for anything said by either the detainee or the Custody Sergeant. It was blank. Paul was relieved. As he suspected, Marie hadn't said anything that would implicate him. The welfare section stated that she was crying uncontrollably but she had declined to see a doctor. Marie was a good girl, he thought, and he didn't want to see her suffer. There was nothing else noted on her record.

Paul took one last swig from the bottle of whisky that he kept returning to the bottom drawer in his desk. It was nearly empty. No more, he thought. He had to drive home and didn't want to be stopped. He hadn't been caught yet in his career and it was too near to the end of his service to risk it. He didn't want to lose his substantial pension. He just wanted to get home; it had been a stressful day.

He thought he would send one last text. "Boss. Just checked custody. All good." It didn't take long for one to come back with a smiley face emoji. Paul smiled. He would wait a little while longer before he left to go home. He reached for a packet of strong mints that sat to the right of his desk. He took one of the mints out of the packet and put it in his mouth. No one would be able to smell any whisky on his breath, he thought.

Just one last refresh of the custody screen to see if Marie was still alright. He pressed the refresh button and saw the list of those in custody. He stopped, and stared at the screen. He looked again to check to see if what he was looking at was correct. He could see that right at the bottom of the list was the name - Dave Harrison. Paul suddenly had a lump in his throat. He felt sick. What on earth had happened? How did he end up getting nicked *too*, he thought. How did anyone know that Harrison was involved? Only Paul knew. Marie didn't know him and no one else knew. He looked again at the screen in disbelief. The words PC Dave Harrison jumped out at him again. He knew that he daren't look at his record as he had no reason to do so. If he did, serious questions as to why he had would follow. He also knew that only Harrison could 'land him in it'; only those two knew what was going on. Paul thought about letting the boss know, but realised if he did it would only make the situation worse. He reached for the bottle again in the bottom of his drawer. He opened it and drained the last drops that were in the bottle. Paul knew PC Dave Harrison was the key to his own exclusion from this worsening situation. He knew he just had to get a message to Harrison somehow. He had to tell him he wasn't to say anything and they would square things off when he was out of custody.

Paul had had a fair amount of whisky by now and the adrenaline was rushing through his body. He knew he shouldn't panic, but he had to make sure his plan was watertight so he wasn't seen to be interfering with Harrison, and anything that was going to happen to him whilst in custody. He reached for his phone. He started typing a text. ". Just need a big favour please. Can you pop in and see Dave whilst he's in the bin. Just write him a note with this on it – 'Square things off tomoz . Coffee on me. Paul' - and put it under his cell door. Cheers." He pressed send. He waited for a reply. It wasn't long before he got a reply. "OK."

Paul sat back in his chair. He didn't know what else to do. He stared straight ahead. There wasn't much else he could do to rescue the situation. He would just have to wait and see what the next day had in store. As long as Marie and Harrison kept their mouths shut all would be well. He knew there was absolutely nothing else he could do that evening. He tidied his desk, turned off his computer screen and locked his drawers. He stood up, slightly unsteady on his feet. He took his jacket from the back of his chair, picked up his phone and his small black rucksack and walked towards the door of the office. He turned off the light and heard the door lock behind him as his left.

Paul was slightly the worse for wear, but had perfected the art of knowing the exact route he had to walk to reach his car parked close to the office, and which was in the same spot every day. The car park was nearly empty as it always was at that time in the late afternoon. The majority of staff who worked at the headquarters complex had gone home for the day, and Paul had done this routine so many times he knew he wouldn't have to speak to anyone before he drove home. He was well over the limit but would never get caught. He got to his car and climbed in. He started it up, turning the fan up to its maximum setting and opened the windows. Another strong mint for the road, he thought, and popped one in his mouth. As the car drove away from the parking bay, he slightly over-revved it. He could see someone look over to his car as he was walking towards it as if startled by the noise. He smiled at them and carried on driving towards the security barrier at the exit to the complex. He looked in his rear-view mirror to see if anyone was coming. There was no one, the barrier opened to let him through and he made his way home.

Chapter 21

Harrison sat in his cell. He was sitting on a blue plastic-covered mattress which was on a concrete bench to one side of the room. It was very stark with nothing else in the cell but a toilet in one corner and a camera in another corner above the door. It could view everywhere in the cell including directly below the door. There was nowhere to hide. There was no privacy at all, and he had to endure this for possibly 24 hours. The thought of it filled him with horror. How would he cope; would he be able to cope at all? It wasn't a pleasant place to be and not one he would have chosen. Of course, Harrison had been in a cell before but not for so long and under completely different circumstances.

It was 6.10pm. He was reading a newspaper he'd been allowed to take to the cell by the Custody Sergeant. She was nice he thought, and even though he was a serving officer who had been arrested, he had been treated with dignity and some sort of respect. Nothing had been proven at this point and he had still to be interviewed. He was hoping because it was early evening he may even be interviewed within the next few hours.

One of the gaolers served his evening meal, the usual low quality rubbish each prisoner received. The all-day breakfast he'd heard so much about and was recommended as the best of a bad choice, was nothing short of terrible. The plastic cutlery he had attempted to use, reflected the quality of the food. He ate hardly any of it. He left it on the floor in the far corner of his cell and had wrapped it up in some toilet paper so that he didn't have to smell it any more.

Harrison looked up from reading his paper. In the corner of his eye, he saw a piece of paper sliding under the door of his cell, folded neatly in half. He stood up from where he was sitting and walked towards the door. He stooped to pick it up. He unfolded it and read what was inside. "Square things off tomorrow. Coffee on me. Paul." Harrison read it repeatedly. The more he did the more his anger grew. "Square things off!" he thought. How dare he try to get out of this! The situation he now found himself in was partly Paul's fault but *he* wasn't the one sitting in a cell. The bloody cheek of it, and all over a coffee, he thought. Harrison was seething. If Paul thought for one moment that by getting him a coffee and trying to 'square things off' he'd get away without any involvement, he'd have another think coming. Who could have slid the note under his cell door? Was it Paul? He would never know.

Harrison walked back to his mattress and sat down. He was so angry about the audacity Paul had shown him, and the nonchalant way he was now treating him that it wasn't time for him to be nice in return. Harrison reached for the custody bell. He pressed the buzzer in order for someone to come to speak to him. "Yes?" said a voice at the end of the speaker. "Can I have solicitor please. I want an interview straight away, and if there is a solicitor available on station then I need them here; it's really important I have one ASAP, please. Thank you." "Okay, I'll see what we can do," replied the female voice of a gaoler.

Harrison sat with his back against the wall. His life would never be the same again and he knew he would never do anything like this again. This was the lowest point in his life and he was not going to go through a repeat of this ordeal. He could hear crying continuing to come from the cell opposite his. This was not a good place to be.

The speaker in his cell crackled into life. "Are you there?" the gaoler asked. "Yep. Go ahead," said Harrison. "You're in luck, there's one just finished a job and is free, so if you want a chat now?" "Sounds good to me." "Fine, I'll come get you and take you for your consultation. I'll be two minutes." "Cheers," said Harrison. At least this was the start of him getting out of there somewhat quicker than he otherwise would have thought.

A short while later the cell door opened and Harrison was escorted to a consultation room within the custody area. On the other side of a grey desk was a man in his mid-forties. He was dressed in a sharp dark blue suit, his shiny black shoes noticeable under the desk. He stood up. "Hello. I'm Ajit. Nice to meet you." The men shook hands. "Hi. Dave Harrison. Good to meet you too." They both sat down on either side of the desk. After going through the pleasantries and Ajit had asked Harrison what happened in general terms about his arrest, Harrison explained all that had occurred that afternoon and how much of a shock it had been to him – and still was.

"Look, Ajit," said Harrison. "I've got a lot to lose here. I'll lose my house, my career and a lot of my friends in the job. I know how others may try to wriggle out of this and it's bloody wrong. I've only been in custody two hours, and already I've had this put under the cell door." He unfolded the note and showed Ajit the piece of paper. "What's this all about"? he said. "Looks like someone's a bit worried. Who's Paul"?

Harrison explained who he was. "Bloody hell. Looks like there's a lot of explaining to do. So how do you want to play this?" Ajit asked. "Well. It's probably best if I tell them the whole truth. I've got nothing to lose and everything to gain. I don't want any more of this shit going on; I mean, it's just plain wrong. I was dragged into this trying to help people out, and although I'm not everyone's cup of tea I haven't got a bad heart. I come across the wrong path many times, but I'm only being me. I haven't done anything really wrong – just trying to help other people out. But look what's happened; I'm in it up to my neck now and others aren't."

Ajit looked at Harrison. "You know you could be looking at doing some time for this? I couldn't say how long but the only way to help yourself is to tell it as it is. If you want, I could speak to the interviewer beforehand and let them know what's coming. They'll give you less of a hard time and you can let them have it all; it's the best way." Harrison looked at Ajit. "Look, don't worry. They'll get it both barrels, the whole bloody lot. Can't wait to see what happens after and the fall-out that comes from it." Harrison had a steely look in his eyes. The determination oozed from his pores; nothing was going to be kept a secret any more. "Anything else, Dave?" "Not at the moment, thanks. I'll just go back to my cell and wait. Do you think I'll be interviewed tonight?" "Look. I'll make some enquiries and hope to get this sorted in the next couple of hours or so. I've had a long day too, but it would be best if we can get you out of here as soon as possible. I'll let you know." "Thanks," said Harrison. "I'd appreciate that."

Harrison opened the door of the consultation room. He beckoned a gaoler to come and escort Ajit, and one walked over from where she was standing behind the custody desk. "All done, thanks," he said to her. "Can I go back in, please?" Harrison walked from the consultation room back to his cell hoping it wouldn't be too long before he was interviewed. He held the piece of paper he had shown Ajit and put it carefully into his pocket. He knew it would prove very useful when he made his disclosure. He knew moreover he was determined Paul wasn't going to get away with anything.

Chapter 22

Michelle was at home. She'd had another long tiring day at work. She had returned home to find her teenage boys who were back from school, on their phones as usual with nothing done around the house. The curtains hadn't been drawn, with all the lights left on illuminating the inside of the house, costing her a fortune. Everyone could see into the rooms at that time of year, and the neighbours were of the nosey type. Whether they were or they weren't, Michelle thought that was the case anyway.

It was 7.13pm. Michelle had just finished dinner and was settling down to watch television when she had an alert sound on her phone. It signalled that there was a message from one of her informants. She took the phone off the small table in the living room next to the sofa where she was sitting and turned down the volume on the TV. She listened to the message. It was from Amy and she was asking Michelle to call her back. Michelle dialled her number and she answered. "Hi Amy. It's Michelle. You alright?" There was crying on the other end of the line. "You okay Amy?" repeated Michelle. There was silence. "Speak to me, Amy." After a short time, Amy answered her. "He's been nicked, hasn't he? *He's been nicked*. Dave. Just tell me he's okay". Michelle fell silent. "He might have been. I don't get involved in that side of things. How do you know?" Amy then went on to say she had a friend who worked with Dave, and that she'd phoned and told her what had happened when Dave was arrested at work. "Listen, Amy. He'll be fine and looked after whilst he's in custody; he'll be interviewed and go through the procedure as everyone else does. I know it's a shock, but it will for the best in the long run 'cos he couldn't carry on doing that sort of stuff forever. It's all thanks to you that he's been caught when he has; don't feel bad about it all. You've done the right thing by telling us what you have; you'll feel better when he's out and you can see him. Whatever you do, don't tell anyone what you have done, meeting us and all that. You okay?" "Thanks Michelle." sputtered Amy. "It's just that I haven't been involved with doing this sort of thing before and he's family as well. It's a lot to take in and I just had to speak to someone. Thank you." Michelle felt a bit more relieved that this was the only issue Amy had with the situation and that she hadn't told anyone what she had done. Michelle had come across this scenario before in her career and it wasn't the easiest of jobs to then resolve. "Listen, Amy. I'm here if you need me. Just call and I'll phone you back. Have a good sleep if you can, tomorrow is another day. Like I said, it'll all be for the best. You've done the most you could have done, and they shouldn't have carried on as they did," she said. "Thank you, Michelle. It means a lot. I'll call you tomorrow once I've spoken to him. Night." "'Bye, Amy." Michelle put the phone back on the table. She had heard this before and knew that everything would be fine. She'd only missed a bit of her programme, so turned the volume up and settled down for the evening.

Chapter 23

It was 8.42pm. Harrison kept looking at his watch. It was getting late and he was really hoping his interview could take place that evening. He didn't really want to spend the night in the cell; it certainly wasn't how he would have planned his day and finishing like this! Suddenly there was a knock at the cell door and he could hear the large heavy lock mechanism turning to open it. The door swung open and standing there was a young detective. "Hiya. Dave?" she said. "I'm DC Elody Kolden. I'm here to take you for interview if you're ready?" Harrison stood up. "Of course. Good to go, thanks." "Great, let's go." Harrison followed her along a corridor to an interview room in the custody area. They went in and she closed the door.

Ajit was already in the room; he was sitting adjacent to a large wooden desk. Elody walked to the far side of the room and sat down gesturing for Harrison to sit down. "I take it you know the procedure and what will happen?" she began, Harrison nodded. He knew all right, he had done this hundreds of times before. The soundproof room had polystyrene tiles all round that deadened any echo that there may have been in the room, so it gave a clipped finish to every word and sentence.

Elody reached for the relevant paperwork she needed for the interview in the drawers positioned next to the table. She placed them on the table in front of Harrison and Ajit and they both acknowledged them. She then went through the formalities of giving Harrison the caution plus all the legal necessities before the interview-proper started. It was a laborious procedure but one she and Harrison had done numerous times before. Elody pressed a button on a small black box that sat to the one side of the desk – it was the interview recording machine.

"Right, Dave. My name is Detective Constable Elody Kolden from the Dorshire Police Anti-Corruption Unit. You understand why you are here?" Harrison replied "Yes." Elody continued. "In your own words tell me why you have been arrested and why this is the case." There was a pause. Harrison looked at Ajit. Ajit nodded as if to tell Harrison to start telling Elody his story.

"It's like this," he began slowly. "I want you to listen very carefully as none of this is made up, I swear it's the truth. I joined Dorshire Police after leaving The Royal Artillery; I served only a few years 'cos I'd had enough of the Army. There were cuts coming and I wasn't enjoying it very much. Joining the police was just the natural thing to do at the time. You know, join a disciplined service and all that; make a new set of friends, have a good laugh, work hard and play hard. I joined up and got posted to Padmouth. It was at a time when the force started doing this type of thing. I told HR it wouldn't be good for me as I'd grown up in the town and knew plenty of people and it could be difficult for me. Loads of people that I grew up with were still about in the town. Most of the people I knew were good but some weren't. One of the ones that wasn't and still isn't is my older brother Mick. You might have heard of him?" "No, sorry Dave, I haven't. I'm not from round that way.

What's he into?" enquired Elody. "He's into drugs and more recently guns. Anyhow, that's not the point at the moment. When I joined up, I didn't really have too much to do with him. I'd been in the Army, knew he was into taking drugs and didn't want much to do with that sort of thing. It was bad news and especially with me joining. I really loved the police and everything that went with it. We had a great team and things were going well. I hadn't been in the job too long when our mum met a new bloke; my real dad had left us for someone else whilst I was still in the Army. My dad was a fireman; Sod! Mum met my step-dad Nigel in a pub one night. He isn't a good person, involved in crime and at a decent level. I warned her about him but she didn't listen. He always had, and still has a lot of money which he's made from drugs. Like I said, I was in the Army when my dad left and was earning good money for my age. Mick was jealous and always wanted money, like the same kind I was on. So when Nigel came along he was sort of encouraged by him to start dealing; it was easy 'cos Nigel had the contacts. It got worse and worse as Mick started making more and more money and becoming more powerful. We've got a younger half-sister who's called Amy; she's amazing and we look after her big time. Really tried to keep her away from Nigel and all his wrong'uns; this includes Mick who doesn't want her getting involved. He makes his money his way, but if it's anything to do with family he'll have them. I think it's because of the way he saw mum get hurt when dad left and he is very protective, and I am too. Anyway, one night a few years ago we went out to a section drink up at one of the lad's houses. Amy is a good-looking girl, and she was only 16 at the time but it was a night out with coppers who you think you could trust. It was late one Saturday night and we were round this bloke's house.

We'd all had a few to drink. We were all in different rooms when Amy came up to me crying. I didn't know what had happened as we were all having a good laugh. I took her outside into the garden and asked her what was wrong. She said a bloke called Jim had been with her alone in a bedroom upstairs, but she trusted him and thought he was different, like a bit quirky and he was a bit of a charmer too. They'd just been chatting, when all of a sudden she said he just lunged towards her and started kissing her. He was more than twice her age. She said that she pushed him off but he just kept trying to force himself on her. She panicked and kicked him hard where it hurts, then just ran out of the room and left him in there and came down and saw me." "Blimey. So what did you do then?" asked Elody. "Well, as you can imagine I was bloody furious, I wanted to knock his block off. Amy was crying and said I couldn't. She said she didn't want anything done about it, but I said I would have it out with him. Trouble was it was bad for the whole team as we were such a tight bunch and it would have broken the team. I had an idea, and so this is where it really all started going wrong. Over the months that I'd been stationed in Padmouth I'd been getting closer to my brother Mick. I knew that he had loads of contacts in Padmouth and he could help me out with bits of information if I helped him out too. It was like a brotherly thing to do, nothing major. Just the odd bit of information that helped him make a few quid and not get caught. I didn't really see what harm it would do if he got me some information and I could get some good arrests for me and the rest of the team. So what happened then was that I decided instead of knocking Jim's head off, I'd tell him, instead of getting Amy to report what he'd done to the police and getting him nicked and everything that went with that, he could help me out by getting information for me. He hadn't long been in a relationship with someone he'd met at training school and that seemed quite strong. Getting him nicked would have lost him everything so I decided to get something out of it for me. It would help my sister too by not getting her to give statements and all that court thing; also Jim would be pleased and the whole thing would be forgotten about - apart from me, Amy and Jim." "I see," said Elody. "Like you were judge and jury and passing sentence all in one evening?" "Yeh, kind of" Harrison agreed. "When we went back into the house I found Jim, got hold of him by the throat and put him against a wall. He knew what he'd done and that I was bloody angry. We were alone in a back room so no one could see us. I said to him that Amy had told me everything and wouldn't report him to anyone. In return for her not reporting him and me not giving him a pasting, was that he had to work for me, doing the odd bit to help me get some information. I told him he wouldn't get caught as long as he played by the rules. If he didn't at any time, Amy would go to the police and report him. To be honest he didn't have much of a choice, so the whole thing started there and has gone on ever since." "So what sort of things has Jim done for you? Like giving you information about what the police have been doing or were planning to do?" Elody probed. "Well yes, all sorts really. From telling me when drugs operations are going to start in the town, to who the main players are, to where and when warrants are going to take place, you know, nothing major that will ever get him in the shit; just stuff that'll help Mick out. He'd never get caught because there will be no trace on any computer; he's not daft. In the last few weeks, though, Mick has been asking me to get him some registration checks done. I've been able to do them via one of

Jim's mates who's called Paul, and it looks like this is how I have ended up in here today." "How come?" pressed Elody. "I was asked by someone I know in the town to get a check done. It was someone who wanted one done on a VW Golf and something to do with shoplifting. I sort of knew Paul from a few years ago but always thought that he was a bit strange; like nobody ever got on with him, a loner. But when I asked Jim about him he said he was alright and could get a check done on a car for me; so I phoned him a few days ago and asked him for a check. It was easy he said and wouldn't come back on me or him, so that's what I did. I gave him the registration and got the check back really quickly; easy." "And what did the car come back as?" asked Elody. "A VW Golf like I was asked about; it went down to a company in Padmouth. I was doing it to see if the car was of interest to the police on the intelligence systems." "Was it?" "No, nothing, so that was all good and I was happy - that's it really. You can see how it all started by Amy not wanting to go to the police because she was scared, me getting something out of it for the team and my brother, and Jim getting something out of it because he kept his career and relationship; and you know the bloody worst thing of all? Jim is now going through the ranks and keeps being promoted. He's a DI and looking for the next rank too. Paul is a Sergeant and hasn't got long until he retires; but not now, I hope." "So who are these people, Dave? I don't know them, but need to check out who they are," said Elody. "Sgt. Paul Slacke did the check; he works in the Traffic Process Unit, and DI Jim Fowler who works with informants; he's only just started there, I think a few weeks ago. He doesn't know too much about it and is finding his feet still." Elody paused. "You mean DI Jim Fowler? The one who was in charge of the Padmouth Taskforce? Him?" "Yep.

Jim Fowler. That's what I mean. No one would ever think that he was bent. I mean he seems like the career cop, married with two children, ex-forces and has a reputation for getting the job done. Well, you can see how he's done it now; he shouldn't be in the job from a long time ago. What he did to my sister is unforgiveable, and to have done what he's done in giving information away via me is terrible too; bent to the core. He's got a reputation for being quite difficult but I think it's so people don't challenge him and question some of his decision-making. He's always been a bit strange, along with Paul. It's like a perfect storm of them knowing each other. I don't really know how they do, but they do." Elody looked at Harrison. "So what do you think will happen to them now that you have told me this? How will we prove what they've done? It's all very well you saying this but it could all be made up to get you out of the mire. It's like maybe a way of deflecting the blame away from you." "Yeh. I get where you are coming from," said Harrison. "But I can give you their personal telephone numbers and you can look at my phone and see when we called or texted each other. That might then tie in with any checks that were made on or before when warrants were done that didn't result in any drug seizures, or when Jim phoned me on duty. I mean, I can give you all that as well as a statement of what's happened, and you might want to get hold of Amy very soon and get a statement off of her. She'll probably know that I've been nicked by now and will be worried stupid. She'll be the first person I speak to when I get out of here. In fact, I'd like to speak to her now, and be the person I'd like to contact to let her know where I am. Can we do that in a moment, please? "Of course," said Elody. "We'll just do this bit first and we'll get you to speak to her on the phone."

Harrison stopped in his tracks. The enormity of what he had just disclosed suddenly dawned on him. He had revealed the secrets of a corrupt network that had been undiscovered for several years. A network that had undone the good work of countless colleagues, some that he knew but the vast majority he didn't. However, the strange thing was that he didn't feel any guilt. He felt a release, as if a weight had been lifted off his shoulders. The burden of guilt that had become a normality and a way of life to him had gone. It was as if he could now return to a way of life free from going behind everyone's backs. He had lost his career and a few friends - but had found freedom. He had been helping out his family but with no benefit to himself. Mick had made money on the back of his efforts, Amy had felt unable to speak out because of fear, and the only other people that had benefitted were colleagues who had been praised for the results they had achieved, and either been heaped with praise or promoted. Where was the justice in all of that? He was the one sitting in an interview room in Midway Police Station, not them.

"Will anyone else get nicked for this?" asked Harrison. Elody looked at him. "It's like this. Someone else has been arrested this afternoon, Dave. It's not either of those two." "Can you tell me who it is, please?" he said. "I don't know if you know her but her name is Marie Solomon." Harrison was dumbstruck. "I've never met her but she's the daughter of one of my mates. How's she ended up being nicked?" "It looks like she's done a check on the VW that you asked Paul to do for you," explained Elody. "What? The cheeky sod. Paul got someone else to do his dirty work for him so that he didn't get caught doing the check. What's he like? The dirty rotten sod. I hope he gets everything that is thrown at him and more. She's completely innocent and doesn't deserve to get drawn into this mess. I hope he does the decent thing and completely exonerates her. Poor girl. I mean, what's going through her head at the minute? Is she here?" he asked. "Yep. She's here too. She's not in a good way." It suddenly became very apparent that the woman Harrison had seen booked in before him and then heard crying was more than likely to be Marie Solomon. What a mess. Of all the people caught up in this, she did not deserve anything like this at all. She had just been doing her job and been nicked.

Elody looked at Ajit. "Well, it looks like we have a job on here. There's obviously a lot for me to do and go away and investigate. Because of the seriousness of what Dave has alleged, I'll be getting my supervisors involved immediately after this interview has concluded. There's a senior ranked officer alleged to be involved in a corruption network in Dorshire Police along with another of a lower rank, but still heavily involved. This has far-reaching implications as you can imagine. In essence, I will ensure that Dave is bailed with conditions, which means that he'll be unable to contact the other defendants. I am pretty sure they'll be arrested very soon so we can stop any further leakage of information, as well as ensuring the investigation is progressed expeditiously. Time is of the essence. I can only thank you for allowing your client to be so open and honest with me during this interview and for which I give him great credit. I hope that this will give him some kudos when it comes to a court process. When we leave this room, I'll ensure that he's able to speak to Amy and we'll make sure that she's safe and well. Is there anything else that either you or Dave would like to say at this time?" Ajit looked at Dave. "Nothing from me, thanks," he said. Harrison looked at Elody. "Not from me, either," he added. "Okay, with that I shall stop the recording." Elody pressed the stop button on the recording device and looked at Ajit and Harrison. "Well, that was different," she observed. "I've never had such an interesting and frank cough from a serving officer!" Harrison looked at her. "I know I've done wrong. I know I've done a *lot* of wrong in fact. Nevertheless, the time has come for me to do the right thing; for me, for Amy, and my colleagues. There are many hard-working people in this force who don't deserve to be treated like that. If this means that a line can start to be drawn under the wrongs that I've done along with those two idiots too, then hopefully the people that I joined to get banged up will all start to get nicked; and I mean my brother Mick, too." With that, they all stood up, shook hands and left the room.

Harrison walked towards the custody desk with Elody. He was dreading talking to Amy but knew that he had to do it. "Can Dave speak to someone to let them know that he is here, please, Sarge?" Elody asked the Custody Sergeant. "Of course, like I said he could," she answered. "Who is it?" "My sister," he replied. "No problem. What's her name and number?" Harrison told her and she dialled the number. Harrison stood in front of the desk. The number rang a few times before being answered. "Hello?" Harrison was nervous. "It's me, Amy." Before he could continue he heard crying on the other end of the phone. "Amy. Please. I've only done what's best for everyone. I've told the truth; it's for the best. *You* need to now, please." There was silence. "Amy?" There was a pause and she asked, "You okay?" "Yep. I'm fine, I just want to get out of here. They'll come round real soon to yours; you'll need to give them a statement and tell them everything that happened with Jim that night. I know it'll be hard for you, but you just have to. It's so important, darling. Just trust me this time, please. I'm begging you." There was further silence. The phone cut off. Harrison stood there with the receiver in his hand, staring straight ahead. He gave it back to the Custody Sergeant. "Thanks, Sarge," he said. She smiled. "No problem," she replied. "We'll pop you back in your cell and I'll speak to Elody. Provided that everything is good for you to go, I'll try and get you out of here as soon as possible." "Thank you," he said. "I appreciate that."

Around the corner of the Custody Desk, a gaoler appeared and beckoned him to go to the corridor where he would be returned to his cell. He turned to Elody. "Thank you for listening, Elody, and for being so good with me. It's made this so much easier." She smiled back at him. He walked towards the gaoler and then a short way down the corridor towards his cell, which was on the left. The cell opposite was quiet. The crying had stopped. Harrison was pleased. If that were Marie Solomon he had seen earlier and heard crying, at least she too would be out of there before long. This part of their ordeal would soon be over and they could get both get out of custody. Out of this nightmare and back to some semblance of normality.

Chapter 24

Elody remained at the Custody Desk once Harrison had left to go back to his cell. She was in conversation with the Custody Sergeant. "Blimey. That was something I never thought I would hear; a copper that had just been nicked talking about corruption and other officers that have been involved, he coughed it good and proper. I'm a bit shocked to be honest Sarge, I mean, in this force, people giving away secrets. It makes you wonder what you are doing the job for." The Custody Sergeant rolled her eyes. She had been in her role a long time and had seen it all. "Nothing much surprises me now," she said. "The only thing that does surprise me, is how many are out there who think they can try and get away with it; very silly." Elody smiled. "I've got to go and speak to my boss now and let him know what's just happened in interview. Once I've done that and he's made a decision about Harrison I'll let you know and then I'll interview Solomon. I'm thinking that it shouldn't take too long, and providing she doesn't come out with anything too complicated as an explanation I'd imagine that they can both be released this evening. I'll let you know." "Fine," the Custody Sergeant replied.

Elody walked a short distance into an anteroom where she could make a call in private. She phoned Keith Catlin. He was expecting her call. He was in charge of the operation to arrest Harrison and Solomon but wasn't expecting what she was about to tell him.

"What the bloody *hell*?" he exclaimed when she outlined to him what Harrison had just told her. "Nothing really surprises me much nowadays, but two officers with rank who are bent. Good God! Whatever next? Right. Get a quick interview out of Solomon and I'll arrange for someone to go round to Amy's house and take a brief statement from her. I need to get it all sorted this evening so that evidence doesn't start disappearing. You know what happens when word gets out, I've seen it before. You alright Elody?" "Yes, Sir. To be honest I'm a bit shocked, but you know, that's life. I'll get an interview done with Solomon and call you back ASAP." "Thanks," he said. "You're doing a cracking job." The phone went down and Elody went back to the Custody Desk.

"Right, Sarge. All good to go from my side. Just a quick interview with Solomon in Cell 6, please, and I'll get her back to you ASAP. Has she got a solicitor?" "Nope, didn't want one; she was upset but no other issues. All good." The Custody Sergeant beckoned for the gaoler as well as asking her to take Elody to Cell 6. The gaoler was sitting down at a desk behind the Custody Sergeant and was looking in her bag for something to eat. A bank of CCTV screens was in front of her showing what was going on in each cell. It was her job to monitor the pictures. She reached into her bag that was on the floor and took out an apple. She leaned back in her seat and looked at the screens. She looked at Cell 6. "Sarge! Oh my God! *Sarge!* Fucking *hell!*" She leapt out of her seat and the two started running down the corridor, closely followed by Elody. They got to the cell door. The gaoler put the key in the lock and opened the door.

She pushed the door and it bumped against an object that prevented it opening with its accustomed ease. She looked round the corner.

Solomon was on the floor behind the cell door and lying on her side, with blood all around her body. Her wrists were slit, and next to her was a fractured piece of the plastic knife she had been given to use with her evening meal; it was scarlet in colour from the blood that had seeped from her wrists. Her eyes were open and she was staring straight ahead; there was little sign of life. Her breathing was shallow and she had gone blue through lack of oxygen. "Oh my God. She's nearly dead. Sarge! *Sarge!*" she screamed. The gaoler reached for the panic alarm and immediately a siren sounded in the custody area. The Custody Sergeant and Elody rushed into the cell behind her; there was panic in their faces. Although trained to deal with this scenario, neither ever thought that they would have to do it. The gaoler checked for a pulse and there was a very slight one. "Get the bloody CPR going!" screamed Elody. "Get her wrists bandaged." Solomon had been on the floor for some time. By now another detective who had been dealing with another prisoner came running down the corridor and rushed into the cell. "I've called an ambulance. Bloody hell. Jesus!" The gaoler crouched down and looked over Marie; she started to cry. The blood had pooled around her wrists and stained both of her rolled-up sleeves. Her hair was thick with blood where it had trickled down and collected in a slight hollow in the concrete floor where her head was resting. She looked peaceful but was still alive, only just, but there was still time to try and save her. They had started CPR and Elody and the gaoler were taking it in turns to try to keep her heart going.

By this time, the custody block was full of staff who had come running to assist once they heard the panic alarm sound. The Custody Sergeant stood up from where she had been crouching and left the cell. "Just get back. Stay away if you don't need to be here," she ordered. She left the gaoler and Elody with Marie. "Stand back, everyone. If you don't work in the custody area you can leave now." Everyone dispersed.

The Custody Sergeant was visibly shaking, this was a major incident in custody; every Custody Sergeant's worst nightmare. The Duty Inspector arrived shortly, followed by the ambulance. The paramedics took over from Elody and the gaoler who had been working on Solomon, and quickly took her away to hospital. She was barely alive, but at least there was hope. For the next few hours, just about everyone who was anyone of rank arrived in the custody block. No one was going anywhere.

Opposite Cell 6 was Cell 7. Harrison lay on his cold, blue plastic mattress; he could hear everything that was going on outside his cell. He heard the commotion when the cell had been opened and Marie had been found. He heard the alarm sound and the frantic activity that followed. He started to cry. He grabbed the small pillow and sobbed uncontrollably into it, his salty tears seeping into the material. His nose filled with mucus and he felt sick. His stomach felt tight and he was shaking. What was all this for, he thought? What has brought this innocent person to a point where they had to try to take their own life? Nothing could ever turn the clock back on what he had done, and now, the horrible consequences that followed, Harrison was in shock. He knew he wouldn't be released from custody that evening. He could not stop thinking of Marie in the cell opposite, and what had driven her to harm herself as she had. He had heard her crying earlier in the evening, and thought when she had stopped it was a good sign. Elody had said that she was not in a good way when brought into custody, but there were no issues that indicated she would do this. Harrison knew the score when it came to the custody booking procedure and what happens thereafter, but for someone who had never experienced it before it was a total shock. The stress placed on people who have never been in trouble with the police is immense, and Marie had succumbed to the pressure. All for what, he wondered. A check on a car registration asked for by Paul Slacke who didn't want to get caught doing it himself. He used someone new to the force to do it for him who probably didn't know any better.

Harrison's contempt for Paul was growing by the minute. He didn't care for him much as a person before all this, and Jim Fowler was the one who put them in contact. Since the incident with Fowler and his sister, there had never been any true trust between them. Their relationship was always based on the fear of Amy reporting Fowler for the sexual assault. Paul Slacke had always had a reputation for being a user who got everyone else to do his work for him, and here was yet another example. This time it had ended like this. Harrison knew that everyone who was involved in this network was culpable, but Paul Slacke was more culpable than the rest. He was the one who had chosen Marie to do the vehicle check as she wouldn't have asked any questions, and she had paid the price. Harrison had already told Elody everything he knew. Now that this had happened he was even more determined that Paul and Jim would not get away with anything, and that he was the one who would take a stand and provide testament to their wrongdoing.

Chapter 25

It was Thursday morning. Martin had just arrived for work. He looked at his watch; it was 7.48am. As usual, he was first in the CO15 office. It was as tidy as he had left it the previous afternoon. He opened all the blinds and turned on the radio. All the desks were cleared as he liked, moreover it looked every part the professional office it was; everything in its place.

Martin sat down at his desk and had just started to look through his paperwork tray to see what he had to do that day when the door to the office opened. In walked Jim. He was unusually early and wearing his familiar stern expression. He walked purposely towards his desk in the far corner of the main office. "Morning, Sir," said Martin. Jim gave a little nod of acknowledgement as he walked past Martin's desk. He was being his customary un-personable self.

Despite the fact Martin knew about the information his handlers had learned about Paul Slacke, he was blissfully unaware of the circumstances that took place yesterday afternoon and the events which had unfolded after the two arrests. This was exactly what should have happened. The CO15 team just collected the intelligence, and it was for others to act upon it and keep him and the team away from the investigation. That said, Michelle had received a call from Amy and she had told Martin of that contact, but it was not for him contact anyone else in turn. The events of that afternoon and evening would be passed to him during the course of the morning.

Martin was mindful that Jim had gone straight to his desk and closed the door to his office. This was slightly unusual, as normally he would keep it open in order to be able to listen to what was being said on the floor in the main office. At the same time, the team started to arrive at work.

It was 7.58am. Michelle, Josh, then Andy and Helen came in and sat down at their desks. They all noticed Jim was already at his desk as there were windows in his small office. They saw the closed door too, but were wary of the fact that Jim could sometimes hear what was going on through the paper thin walls.

Jim logged onto his computer. He clicked onto the internal Dorshire Police telephone directory. With a degree of urgency, he started typing PS Paul Slacke. He needed to speak to him straightaway about what had happened the day before. Jim had been at home and had cut himself off from what was going on at work. Paul had reassured him about what had occurred, but a face-to-face meeting would ensure Paul could let him know exactly what had happened. Jim was careful not to have anything written down that could possibly incriminate him. He had been involved in all sorts of investigations long enough to know how suspects came to be caught and he wasn't about to start landing himself in it now.

He phoned Paul's number. It rang and rang. There was no reply. This wasn't unusual for him; he was generally five or ten minutes late for work. Besides, Paul would see a missed call from him and would phone him back he hoped. Jim had a busy day ahead as he still had the Surveillance Commissioner's visit to prepare for, and although he had gotten some of the preparation done working from home the day before, he still had much to do. Working from home was never a great move for him. Lorraine hadn't been at work the day before either, and she'd taken the Thursday off as well as Friday so they could spend some time together. Jim had had a stressful few weeks, and although she had planned for them to go for a nice walk and have a spot of lunch somewhere, he'd made his mind up he would have a different idea, and decided to cancel his days off to be able to get on with his preparations. As he had suspected, Lorraine had annoyed him whilst he was doing his work at home and had left to stay with her sister last night to let him get on with it. She said that she would be back when he returned home after work today. She better had, he thought. He'd had to cook his own dinner the previous night.

Jim sat at his desk in his office waiting for Paul to phone him. He looked at his watch; it was 8.06hrs. He noticed through the glass that Martin had started the daily team meeting. He had the door closed but was reluctant to open it just in case Paul phoned. He could hear muffled voices through the walls but nothing was audible.

Martin was chairing the meeting. He knew he had to be so careful with what the team would be saying regarding the informants they had been managing that week without Jim's knowledge. The team were only too aware of it as well. As the week had progressed, they had become a bit more used to how Martin was managing affairs and so far everything had worked perfectly.

The team gathered for their daily meeting. "So, morning, guys. Hope everyone is well. Just a few things to go through before we go round to see what everyone has planned for the day. It's Friday, so please make sure the cars are cleaned and fuelled ready for next week. Make sure too that your informants are fully aware of who is taking calls this weekend and if they've been tasked to get any information." At that point, he heard the handle on the door of Jim's office turn. He looked round to see if Jim was coming out, but he wasn't. He had opened the door but had returned to his desk.

Martin continued. "Good. So Andy. What have you got planned for today?" "Well, I've got a call to put into Lee Heaveney again just to make sure he's okay..." Andy was cut short. "Right!" Jim's voice boomed from his office. "I want him sacked. That fella gives us nothing and wants too much in return. We're carrying far too much risk trying to manage him whilst he's in prison. Too much jeopardy. Phone him and tell him he's finished. Sort out any money that's owed to him and then that's it." There was silence in the office. "Sure boss," agreed Andy. "So then I've got to meet Kayne Woollery with Josh. He's..." Again Jim's voice bellowed out. "Nope. No more meetings with that waster. We get absolutely nothing from that idiot. He just meets us and it's all on his terms. It's got jeopardy written all over it. Get rid today, please. It's the last meeting with him. No money. Get *rid*." Andy was dumbstruck. He looked at Martin. Jim could just see Martin as he smirked. His blood boiled and he snapped. "Martin. Get that bloody smirk off your face and get in here!" he shouted. Martin turned around and looked at him. Martin smirked again.

Just then, Jim's phone rang. It was Paul Slacke's number on the screen. "Right. Give me two minutes and get your arse in here," he demanded and slammed the door. There was an uncomfortable silence in the office. Everyone looked at each other. This was yet another low point in the recent history of the team. The DI had been shouting at his Sergeant. This was not something they'd ever seen before, and not part of the modern ways of of Dorshire Police.

There was a knock on the office door. Michelle got up and opened it. Outside was DCI Keith Catlin and two uniformed officers. "Morning, Michelle. Can you stand aside, please? We need to come in." The three walked in purposefully and went straight to Jim's office in the far corner of the room. Keith turned the handle and opened the door. Jim sat at his desk, on the phone to Paul. "Two seconds gents," he said. "Okay, I'll see you there at 9.30." He hung up. "Sorry, Keith," he went on. "Morning mate. How can I help you?" The taller of the two uniformed officers stepped forward in front of Keith. "DI Jim Fowler, I'm arresting you for Misconduct in a Public Office. You do not have to say anything, but it may harm your defence if you do not mention when questioned something you later rely on in court. Anything you do say may be given in evidence." Jim just looked straight ahead. He was in shock, stunned by the words he had uttered himself so many times, but were now being said to him. He sat back in his chair. "You sure, guys? This is some sort of joke, right? I mean, you've got the right person? - the right Jim Fowler? What am I have supposed to have done?" "Jim. There's the procedure to go through, as you know," said Keith. "We'll get you into custody at Midway and you will be interviewed there. Let's get going." Jim stood up and walked round to the front of his desk. He was shaking. The arresting officer got his handcuffs out and offered them to him. Keith chipped in. "Not necessary this time, thanks, lads." "Let's go," ordered Keith. The four walked out of Jim's office and across the floor between the desks and towards the office door.

The team had seen everything that had gone on and heard every word said. They were in shock too. Never had one of their own, let alone their boss, been arrested. They looked at Jim who was expressionless as he crossed the floor. He walked past Martin's desk and looked at Martin. Martin smiled at him; he mouthed, "You'll pay for this." Jim stared back. He knew his time was up but didn't know how this had happened or what was behind his arrest.

Jim and those accompanying him left the office. There was a stunned silence. The team looked at each other across their desks. By now, they had each guessed what might have been at the root of their reporting during the previous few days. They were an experienced team and knew how the system worked; they'd had training on corruption and how it can manifest itself. The reporting they had been providing from their informants had been shared between themselves, and they were fully aware something significant was amiss. The level of detail they had obtained from their sources was too serious and too coincidental in its timing, it just had to lead somewhere. That somewhere had happened right in front of them. What they didn't know was how the last twenty-four hours had unfolded which had led to Jim's arrest, and who else was involved.

Martin broke the silence. "Guys. What can I say? We've just witnessed our boss getting nicked. I have never seen that before, and hope I never do again, but what I will say is this. Please do not repeat any of this to anyone until I have spoken to Keith Catlin in order to get the full circumstances behind it. We've accomplished our bit and you've all done brilliantly. What we don't want, is a witch-hunt by anyone associated with Jim to try an un-nerve us until I know what's happened. Everyone clear?" They all nodded. "Right. Where was I before the interruption?" They all laughed nervously. Martin was cool. Nothing really phased him and he continued as if it were just another day, which it was. Martin had no time for Jim, nor did the rest of the team; this hadn't really surprised him, knowing Jim's reputation.

"So Josh. Who did you want to meet today?" "Well, I'd really like to meet Kayne Woolery, please! Think there might be some mileage left in him yet. I'll also phone Lee Heaveney and touch base with him. Then I'll see what everyone else has got on and if there's anything they need me to do." "Thanks ," said Martin. The rest of the team then went through the work they had on that day. Michelle and Helen had to meet Amy to make sure that she was alright, and Andy had to meet Woolery with Josh and catch up with some paperwork. "Breakfast, anyone?" The team laughed as they all got up and headed for the door.

Chapter 26

It was mid-morning and Martin still hadn't received a call from Keith Catlin. He was half-expecting it due to the arrest that had taken place in the CO15 office that morning, but knew these things took time to deal with. Martin understood there were things happening behind the scenes, and that others had to get on with their work. It was not for him to start interfering; it wouldn't make any difference anyway. The team had enjoyed a relaxed breakfast and were in good spirits. Despite their boss having been arrested in front of them, everyone could sense an air of relief in the office. Jim had been arrested and whatever the outcome of the investigation, it was highly unlikely that he would be returning to the team in the short-term. Whatever he would say in interview meant he would be bailed and be off work for some time. Martin had his fingers crossed.

Martin was at his desk nervously waiting for his phone to ring. The team was out of the office, apart from Ellie who had buried herself as usual in her work. Ellie hated with a passion anything that upset the normal workings of the team and the arrest of Jim had unsettled her. Martin thought it best to leave her to her own thoughts.

Martin's desk phone suddenly rang. It was Keith. "You okay boss?" said Martin. "Yep. Fine. Have you got five minutes to spare, please?

I've got an update for you about all that's been happening today and yesterday. In fact, quite a lot has been going on." "Yes, Sir. I'll be over in ten minutes." "Thanks. See you soon," said Keith. There was relief on Martin's face. He'd had a stressful week keeping the informants safe and what they were reporting on behind Jim's back, but it seemed that he had been vindicated. He knew that corrupt officers strike at any level and those of higher rank usually do not fall under any suspicion. He was looking forward to hearing about what had happened and how Jim had ended up being nicked.

Martin grabbed his jacket and headed for the office door. "I don't know how long I'll be," he said to Ellie. "I'm off to see Keith in Anti-Corruption." "See you later," said Ellie. She didn't want to get drawn into any conversation about anything to do with the arrest or the events of the morning; it was just her way.

Martin headed down the stairs and out into the car park. The fresh morning air filled his lungs, and with a feeling of satisfaction made his way across the back of the main headquarters building towards where the Anti-Corruption Unit was based. For the first time in a few weeks, he had a skip in his step. Life was feeling a lot better again and the weekend was just around the corner. It would definitely be a good one.

It didn't take long for him to reach what was a modern and imposing building and he went straight up the stairs to Keith's office. The door to the office was already slightly open and he peered round the door. He could see Keith sitting at his desk. "Can I come in, boss?" he asked. "Yes; take a seat," said Keith. "You okay?" "Yep. Think so," said Martin.

Keith sat back in his chair whilst Martin sat down in the chair in front of Keith's desk. "There's a great deal that's happened in the last few days, in fact not only in the last few days but in the last 24 hours which you won't be aware of. I take it you don't know about how things have worked out since yesterday?" "No, Sir. We put the info in about the telephone numbers and left you to it; that's the way it should work, shouldn't it?" "Yes, you're quite right. So it's happened like this. You gave us the numbers and the background to Dave Harrison, and everything then just worked like clockwork. Dave got nicked along with Marie Solomon who works in Paul Slacke's office. In interview, Dave coughed it all and gave us everything. He told us about Jim Fowler and how he ended up becoming involved in the network; Jim had sexually assaulted Amy and she was too scared to report him to the police. Marie had nothing to do with it so it must have been Paul Slacke who asked her to do the check on the car. By the way, Paul was arrested at his desk this morning at the same time as Jim was nicked; but there's something else you need to know. Marie tried to commit suicide in her cell; this was before the interview, and she's not in a good way. She's in hospital being patched up, however the signs are good that she'll pull through. We will interview her in good time. Dave has provided a statement against Jim and Paul and so has Amy. We've got all the telephone evidence showing communication at the relevant times between Dave, Paul and Jim which matches the time of the check on the car, and we also seized Jim's and Paul's own phones to see if there's anyone else involved. Dave told us that he'd had a note slipped under his cell door on behalf of Paul, but up to now we haven't been able to find out who was responsible for that. We're still checking the cameras in the cellblock to see if we can identify who went to Dave's cell. We're also checking the electronic swipes to see who was in the cellblock at the time, but it's going to take a bit of work to narrow it down. Then we have to prove who it is and that they are involved. Tricky one. There's still someone out there who is part of the group, so if you can find out who it is please, that would be great. No pressure! So that's about where we are with it all at the moment. Any questions?"

Martin took his time to answer. "So what you are saying is that the network has been broken up, based on what the CO15 team has come up with in the last few days. There are certain things that have just started falling into place." "Like what?" enquired Keith. "Like Jim coming into the team and trying to get rid of certain informants; also trying to remove people like me from the team as maybe we know too much — and certainly more than him about running informants. Like him also protecting certain people in this organisation who were obviously now in hindsight, very important to his network, not to mention him trying to be promoted. I mean, he's one *dirty* dog. I hope he's looking at doing a decent stretch inside for what he did to Amy and Marie, let alone what he has done to the credibility of this force. I really feel for those two. They've been caught up in all of this mess and they haven't done anything wrong. I hope those two idiots can go to bed and sleep well tonight 'cos of what they've done to Amy and Marie. Disgusting! Paul Slacke has always been a liability to this force and I'm glad he's had his comeuppance; terrible. Look Sir, can I ask a big favour, please?" "Sure. So what's that then? Maybe a pay rise or promotion?" Keith said with an air of sarcasm in his voice. "No, not quite," replied Martin. "It's just that the team has been under the microscope for some time, what with the next round of cuts coming in the force. This investigation may have just saved the team by showing what they are really worth. There is a lot of experience in that team and they are as straight as you will ever find. If you could somehow get to mention us to ACC Rick Donning to make sure he doesn't forget us in the next round of cuts I'd be very grateful. For Christ's sake - we've just captured three bent coppers for him!" Keith smiled. "It's the least I can do. Absolutely cracking job; just goes to show the value of well-placed snouts. Always has done and always will do." Martin stood up, leaned across the desk and shook Keith's hand. "Thanks, Sir. Top man." He turned and made his way to the door. "That Jim's a proper wrong-un, you know. There's a bit more to him which I'll tell you about another time. Believe you me, this force will be a much better place without him." With that, he closed the door behind him.

Martin made his way across the car park back towards the CO15 office. He had a warm feeling inside him of a job well done. He couldn't wait to tell the team what had happened, and that the results of their hard work and risks they had taken had come to fruition. As he walked towards the door to the building, he saw ACC Rick Downing walking in front of him. He had never met him before but recognised his face from the force internal media releases. It was a bit of a chance encounter but Martin was always one to seize the moment. "Sir. Mr Donning," he said. The ACC turned around and saw Martin walking towards him. "Yes. What's up?" he asked. "Sir. Have you got five minutes, please?" requested Martin. "Of course. What can I help you with?" Martin introduced himself, and as he did so the ACC started smiling. "Oh, nice to meet you, Martin. I think I know what this is all about. Cracking job. You and the team should be very proud of yourselves. I've been kept updated by Keith as the job has developed this week, a great result." The ACC was very pleased; albeit that bent coppers had been nicked in the force. "So it's a bit cheeky and premature of me to ask but in the next round of cuts do you..." The ACC interrupted Martin. "Look, Martin. I know it's a cracking result, but it's a bit early for that sort of talk and that type of decision to be made; in the fullness of time all will be worked through. What I can tell you though is, this won't have done the team any harm at all. It has shown the value of what we have in the unit, and we as a force would be foolish to think that by discarding it we would be doing ourselves any favours in the long run." "Sir, thank you for that. All I would say is that you know that we will always do our best. Thank you for your time and hope you have a great day." "Thanks, Martin. Nice to meet you and hope we can have a coffee together sometime."

With that, the two men went on their way. The ACC no doubt going to an important meeting, Martin going back to the office to brief his team.

Chapter 27

The CO15 team were waiting in the office. It was 10.48am and there was an air of excitement in the room. There hadn't been such a feeling for a few weeks. Michelle was laughing about something that Andy had just said and Josh was twirling a martial-arts stick he kept in the office. There was an end-of-term feeling about the place. The team were chatting so much that they didn't hear the stairs creaking as Martin climbed them and approached the office door. He heard the laughter and it made him smile. *This is the way it should be*, he thought.

He used his swipe card to open the door and enter the office. As he did so, there was a cheer and the team laughed. "Look, guys. Take a seat and I'll explain all." The team sat down at their desks and listened intently as Martin explained the details with which Keith had just updated him. "As you know, Jim got nicked this morning along with Paul Slacke. In addition, PC Dave Harrison from Padmouth was arrested and has now been bailed. An administrative assistant called Marie Solomon was arrested too; she worked for Paul, and it looks like she did the check on the car for him. She isn't in a good way, having tried to take her own life whilst in custody; not good, but Keith will let me know how she gets on; let's hope she makes a full recovery. You'll be pleased to know that Jim won't be coming back here any time soon. I hope they'll get something to stick and he'll be sent down, so I think we all now know why he has been acting the way he has since he came to this team. In my opinion it looks like he was trying to undermine not only me but the team as well, *and* the informants we have on the books. It's only down to your commitment and professionalism that we stood up to him and showed what this team is made of. The value of informants, eh? Never underestimate a well-run snout and what they can give you. Tremendous work!"

Martin looked at the team and knew what he had in them. A close-knit group of professionals who always gave everything, even in the face of a corrupt so-called leader. "Anyone got anything to say?" invited Martin. The team looked back at him. There was silence. "Nothing at all?" he said. Still nothing. "Okay. Well if there's nothing else, then I suggest a late breakfast!" Everyone laughed. They all stood up and walked towards the door. As they did so, they smiled at each other. "Think that there was just a bit too much jeopardy in this job for Jim," said Michelle. "It's definitely been Jeopardy Jim for the last few weeks for sure," said Martin as they all left the office and went for breakfast.

Epilogue

Marie recovered from her injuries and left hospital a few weeks later. She made a statement against Paul Slacke but left the force, and is still receiving treatment for mental health issues.

Amy gave a statement against Jim Fowler.

Dave admitted his offence and was convicted at court. He received a suspended sentence. He is now a courier driver in Padmouth.

Paul Slacke admitted his offence and received an eight- month custodial sentence. He is still drinking heavily.

Jim Fowler denied everything but was convicted and received a thirteen-month sentence for Misconduct in a Public Office and a two-year sentence for Sexual Assault, which he is serving to run concurrently. Lorraine divorced him.

The person who slipped the note under the cell door for Harrison was never identified.

The CO15 team is still waiting to hear whether they will be involved in the next round of cost-cutting in Dorshire.

Acknowledgements

I wish to express my heart-felt thanks to all those friends and family who have supported me through the good and the more challenging times and have always been there for me.
In particular Ali and her reader group, Janet for proof-reading the book, Barbs @809design.com for the cover-design and to my parents for the time and effort they took during the COVID-19 lockdown to painstakingly copyedit the manuscript.

To my wife Heather for her seemingly endless patience, tolerance, love and support. To the team, once again thank you.

There are those who have committed wrongdoing who will never sleep well. Thank you also for having made those unfortunate enough to have met you stronger people.

Printed in Great Britain
by Amazon